"I WANT MY HUSBAND BACK!"

Mrs. Vail got her bag and opened it and took out an envelope. "He didn't come home Sunday night, and yesterday this came in the mail."

It was an ordinary off-white envelope. The flap had been cut clean with a knife or opener, no jagged edges. I handed it to Wolfe, and he removed the contents, a folded sheet of cheap bond paper, the kind you get in scratch pads. He held it to his left, so I could read it too. This is what it said:

> We have got your Jimmy safe and sound. We haven't hurt him any and you can have him back all in one piece for $500,000 if you play it right and keep it strictly between you and us. We mean strictly. If you try any tricks, you'll never see him again.

The Final Deduction

by Rex Stout

A Nero Wolfe Mystery

BANTAM BOOKS

TORONTO · NEW YORK · LONDON · SYDNEY · AUCKLAND

*This low-priced Bantam Book
has been completely reset in a type face
designed for easy reading, and was printed
from new plates. It contains the complete
text of the original hard-cover edition.*
NOT ONE WORD HAS BEEN OMITTED

THE FINAL DEDUCTION

*A Bantam Book / published by arrangement with
The Viking Press, Inc.*

PRINTING HISTORY

Viking edition published October 1961
Dollar Mystery Guild edition published February 1962
Bantam edition published March 1963
2nd printing . . . . August 1963   3rd printing . . . . September 1968
4th printing . . . . September 1969
New Bantam edition published October 1970
2nd printing . . . . . . October 1974   3rd printing . . . . May 1981
4th printing . . . . November 1985

*All rights reserved.
Copyright © 1955 by Rex Stout.
This book may not be reproduced in whole or in part, by
mimeograph or any other means, without permission.
For information address: The Viking Press, Inc.,
40 W. 23 St., New York, NY 10010.*

ISBN 0-553-76310-5

Published simultaneously in the United States and Canada

1

"Your name, please?"

I asked her only as a matter of form. Having seen her picture in newspapers and magazines at least a dozen times, and having seen her in person at the Flamingo and other spots around town, I had of course recognized her through the one-way glass in the door as I went down the hall to answer the doorbell, though she wasn't prinked up for show. There was nothing dowdy about her brown tailored suit or fur stole or the hundred-dollar pancake on her head, but her round white face, too white there in daylight, which could be quite passable in a restaurant or theater lobby, could have stood some attention. It was actually flabby, and the rims of her eyes were red and swollen. She spoke.

"I don't think . . ." She let it hang a moment, then said, "But you're Archie Goodwin."

I nodded. "And you're Althea Vail. Since you have no appointment, I'll have to tell Mr. Wolfe what you want to see him about."

"I'd rather tell him myself. It's very confidential and very urgent."

I didn't insist. Getting around as I do, and hearing a lot of this and that, both true and false, I had a guess on what was probably biting her, and if that was it I would enjoy watching Wolfe's face as she spilled it, and hearing him turn her down. So I admitted her. The usual routine with a stranger who has no appointment is to leave him or her on the stoop while I go and tell Wolfe, but I can make exceptions, and it was a raw windy day for late April, so I took her to the front room, the first door on your left when you are inside, returned to the hall, and went to the second door on the left, to the office.

Wolfe was on his feet over by the big globe, glaring at

a spot on it. When I had gone to answer the bell he had
been glaring at Cuba, but he had shifted to Laos.

"A woman," I said.

He stuck with Laos. "No," he said.

"Probably," I conceded. "But she says it's urgent and
confidential, and she could pay a six-figure fee without
batting an eye. Her name is Althea Vail. Mrs. Jimmy
Vail. You read newspapers thoroughly, so you must
know that even the *Times* calls him Jimmy. Her eyes are
red, presumably from crying, but she is now under control. I don't think she'll blubber."

"No!"

"I didn't leave her on the stoop because of the weather.
She's in the front room. I have heard talk of her, and I
understand that she is prompt pay."

He turned. "Confound it," he growled. He took in a
bushel of air through his nose, let it out through his
mouth, and moved. Behind his desk he stood, a living
mountain, beside his oversized chair. He seldom rises to
receive a caller, woman or man, but since he was already
on his feet it would take no energy to be polite, so why
not? I went and opened the connecting door to the front
room, told Mrs. Vail to come, presented her, and con-
voyed her to the red leather chair near the end of Wolfe's
desk. Sitting, she gave the stole a backward toss, and it
would have slid to the floor if I hadn't caught it. Wolfe
had lowered his 285 pounds into his chair and was scowling at her, his normal attitude to anyone, especially a
woman, who had the gall to come uninvited to the old
brownstone on West 35th Street, his house, expecting him
to go to work.

Althea Vail put her brown leather bag on the stand at
her elbow. "First," she said, "I'd better tell you how I got
here."

"Not material," Wolfe muttered.

"Yes it is," she declared. It came out hoarse, and she
cleared her throat. "You'll see why. But first of all it has
to be understood that what I'm going to tell you is absolutely in confidence. I know about you, I know your reputation, or I wouldn't be here, but it has to be definite
that this is in *complete confidence.* Of course I'm going to
give you a check as a retainer, and perhaps I should do

that before . . ." She reached to the stand for her bag. "Ten thousand dollars?"

Wolfe grunted. "If you know about me, madam, you should know that that's fatuous. If you want to hire me to do a job, what is it? If I take it, a retainer may or may not be required. As for confidence, nothing that you tell me will be revealed unless it involves a crime which I am obliged, as a citizen and a licensed private detective, to report to authority. I speak also for Mr. Goodwin, who is in my employ and who—"

"It does involve a crime. Kidnaping is a crime."

"It is indeed."

"But it must *not* be reported to authority."

My brows were up. Seated at my desk, my chair swiveled to face her, I crossed off the guess I had made. Apparently I wouldn't get to watch Wolfe's face while a woman asked him to tail her husband, or to hear him turn her down. He was speaking.

"Certainly kidnaping is unique. The obligation not to withhold knowledge of a major crime must sometimes bow to other considerations, for instance saving a life. Is that your concern?"

"Yes."

"Then you may trust our discretion. We make no firm commitment, but we are not fools. I suppose you have been warned to tell no one of your predicament?"

"Yes."

"Then I was wrong. How you got here is material. How did you?"

"I phoned a friend of mine, Helen Blount, who lives in an apartment on Seventy-fifth Street, and arranged it with her. The main entrance to the apartment house is on Seventy-fifth Street, but the service entrance is on Seventy-fourth Street. I phoned her at half past ten. I told my chauffeur to have my car out front at half past eleven. At half past eleven I went out and got in my car and was driven to my friend's address. I didn't look behind to see if I was being followed because I was afraid the chauffeur would notice. I got out and went into the apartment house—the men there know me—and I went to the basement and through to the service entrance on Seventy-fourth Street, and Helen Blount was there in her car, and

I got in, and she drove me here. So I don't think there's the slightest chance that they know I'm seeing Nero Wolfe. Do you?"

Wolfe turned to me. "Archie?"

I nodded. "Good enough. Hundred to one. But if someone's waiting in Seventy-fifth Street to see her home and she never shows, he'll wonder. It would be a good idea to go back before too long and enter on Seventy-fourth and leave on Seventy-fifth. I would advise it."

Her red-rimmed eyes were at me. "Of course. What would be too long?"

"That depends on how patient and careful he is, and I don't know him." I glanced at my wrist. "It's twenty-five after twelve. You got there a little more than half an hour ago. You could reasonably be expected to stay with your friend quite a while, hours maybe. But if he knows you well enough to know that your friend Helen Blount lives there he might call her number and ask for you and be told that you're not there and you haven't been there. I have never known a kidnaper personally, but from what I've read and heard I've got the impression they're very sensitive."

She shook her head. "He won't be told that. Helen told her maid what to say. If anyone asks for me, or her either, he'll be told that we're busy and can't come to the phone."

"Good for you. But there's Helen Blount. She knows you came to see Nero Wolfe."

"She doesn't know what for. That's all right, I can trust her. I *know* I can." Her eyes went back to Wolfe. "So that's how I got here. When I leave I have to go to my bank, and then I'll go back to Seventy-fourth Street." It was coming out hoarse again, and she cleared her throat and coughed. "It's my husband," she said. She got her bag and opened it and took out an envelope. "He didn't come home Sunday night, and yesterday this came in the mail."

Her chair was too far away for her to hand it to Wolfe without getting up, and of course he wouldn't, so I did. It was an ordinary off-white envelope with a typewritten address to Mrs. Jimmy Vail, 994 Fifth Avenue, New York City, no zone number, and was postmarked BRYANT STA

APR 23, 1961 11:30 P.M. Sunday, day before yesterday. The flap had been cut clean with a knife or opener, no jagged edges. I handed it to Wolfe, and after a glance at the address and postmark he removed the contents, a folded sheet of cheap bond paper, also off-white, five by eight unfolded, the kind you get in scratch pads. He held it to his left, so I could read it too. We no longer have it, but from some shots I took of it the next day I can have it reproduced for you to look at. It may tell you what it told Wolfe about the person who typed it. Here it is:

> We have got your Jimmy safe and sound. We haven't hurt him any and you can have him back all in one piece for $500,000 if you play it right and keep it strictly between you and us. We mean strictly. If you try any tricks you'll never see him again. You'll get a phone call from Mr. Knapp and don't miss it.

Wolfe dropped it on the desk pad and turned to Althea Vail. "I can't forgo," he said, "an obvious comment. Surely this is humbug. Kidnaping is a desperate and dangerous operation. It's hard to believe that a man committed to it, a man who has incurred its mortal risks, could be in a mood to make a pun—that in choosing an alias to use on the phone, for himself in his role as kidnaper, he would select 'Knapp.' It must be flummery. If not, if this thing is straightforward"—he tapped the paper with a finger—"the man who wrote it is most extraordinary. Is your husband a practical joker?"

"No." Her chin had jerked up. "Are you saying it's a joke?"

"I suggested the possibility, but I also suggested an alternative, that you have a remarkable man to deal with. Have you heard from Mr. Knapp?"

"Yes. He phoned yesterday afternoon, my listed number. I had told my secretary that I expected the call, and she listened on an extension. I thought she might as well because she opens my mail and she had read that thing."

"What did he say?"

"He told me what to do. I'm not going to tell you. I'm going to do exactly what he said. I don't need you for that. What I need you for, I want my husband back.

Alive. I know they may have killed him already, I know that, but—" Her chin had started to work, and she pressed her lips together to stop it. She went on, "If they have, then I'll want to find them if the police and the FBI don't. But on the phone yesterday that man said he was all right, and I believe him. I *must* believe him!"

She was on the edge of the chair. "But don't kidnapers often kill after they get the money? So they can't be traced or recognized? Don't they?"

"That has happened."

"Yes. That's what I need you for. Doing what he said, getting the money to them, I'll do that myself, there's nothing you can do about that. I've told my banker I'm coming to get the money this afternoon, and I'll do—"

"Half a million dollars?"

"Yes. And I'll do exactly what that man said, but that's all I can do, and I want him back. I want to be sure I'll get him back. That's what I need you for."

Wolfe grunted. "Madam. You can't possibly mean that. You are not a nincompoop. How could I conceivably proceed? The only contact with that punster or an accomplice will be your delivery of the money, and you refuse to tell me anything about it. Pfui. You can't possibly mean it."

"But I do. I do! That's why I came to *you!* Is there anything you can't do? Aren't you a genius? How did you get your reputation?" She took a checkfold from her bag and slipped a pen from a loop. "Will ten thousand do for a retainer?"

She had a touch of genius herself, or it was her lucky day, asking him if there was anything he couldn't do and waving a check at him. He leaned back, closed his eyes, and cupped the ends of the chair arms with his hands. I expected to see his lips start moving in and out, but they didn't; evidently this one was too tough for any help from the lip routine. Mrs. Vail opened the checkfold on the stand at her elbow, wrote, tore the check from the fold, got up and put it on Wolfe's desk, and returned to the chair. She started to say something, and I pushed a palm at her. A minute passed, another, and two or three more, before Wolfe opened his eyes, said, "Your notebook, Archie," and straightened up.

I got my notebook and pen. But instead of starting to dictate he closed his eyes again. In a minute he opened them and turned to Mrs. Vail.

"The wording is important," he said. "It would help to know how *he* uses words. You will tell me exactly what he said on the phone."

"No, I won't." She was emphatic. "You would try to do something, some kind of trick. You'd have Archie Goodwin do something. I know he's clever and you may be a genius, but I'm not going to risk that. I told that man I would do exactly what he told me to, and do it alone, and I'm not going to tell you. What wording is important? Wording of what?"

Wolfe's shoulders went up an eighth of an inch and down again. "Very well. His voice. Did you recognize it?"

She stared. "Recognize it? Of course not!"

"Had you any thought, any suspicion, that you had ever heard it before?"

"No."

"Was he verbose, or concise?"

"Concise. He just told me what to do."

"Rough or smooth?"

She considered. "Neither one. He was just—matter-of-fact."

"No bluster, no bullying?"

"No. He said this would be my one chance and my husband's one chance, but he wasn't bullying. He just said it."

"His grammar? Did he make sentences?"

She flared. "I wasn't thinking of grammar! Of course he made sentences!"

"Few people do. I'll rephrase it: Is he an educated man? 'Educated' in the vulgar sense, as it is commonly used."

She considered again. "I said he wasn't rough. He wasn't vulgar. Yes, I suppose he is educated." She gestured impatiently. "Isn't this wasting time? You're not enough of a genius to guess who he is or where he is from how he talked. Are you?"

Wolfe shook his head. "That would be thaumaturgy, not genius. When and where did you last see your husband?"

"Saturday morning, at our house. He left to drive to the country, to our place near Katonah, to see about things. I didn't go along because I wasn't feeling well. He phoned Sunday morning and said he might not be back until late evening. When he hadn't come at midnight I phoned, and the caretaker told me he had left a little after eight o'clock. I wasn't really worried, not really, because sometimes he takes a notion to drive around at night, just anywhere, but yesterday morning I *was* worried, but I didn't want to start calling people, and then the mail came with that thing."

"Was he alone when he left your place in the country?"

"Yes. I asked the caretaker."

"What is your secretary's name?"

"My secretary? You jump around. Her name is Dinah Utley."

"How long has she been with you?"

"Seven years. Why?"

"I must speak with her. You will please phone and tell her to come here at once."

Her mouth opened in astonishment. It snapped shut. "I will not," she said. "What can she tell you? She doesn't know I've come to you, and I don't want her to. Not even her. I trust her absolutely, but I'm not going to take *any* chances."

"Then there's your check." Wolfe pointed to it, there on his desk. "Take it and go." He made a face. "I must have some evidence of your bona fides, however slight. I do know you are Mrs. Jimmy Vail, since Mr. Goodwin identifies you, but that's all I know. Did that thing come in the mail and did you get a phone call from Mr. Knapp? I have only your unsupported word. I will not be made a party to some shifty hocus-pocus. Archie. Give Mrs. Vail her check."

I got up, but she spoke. "It's no hocus-pocus. My God, hocus-pocus? My husband—they'll kill him! My not wanting anyone to know I've come to you, not even my secretary—isn't that right? If you expect her to tell you what he said on the phone, she won't. I'll tell her not to."

"I won't ask her." Wolfe was curt. "I'll merely ask her how he said it. If you have been candid, and I have no reason to think you haven't, you have no valid objection to my speaking with her. As for her knowing that you have come to me, Mr. Knapp will soon know that himself —or I hope he will."

She gawked. *"He* will know? How?"

"I'll tell him." He turned. "Archie. Can we get an advertisement in the evening papers?"

"Probably, the late editions," I told him. "The *Post* and *World-Telegram,* we can try. The *Gazette,* yes, with Lon Cohen's help." I was back in my chair with notebook and pen. "Classified?"

"No. It must be conspicuous. Two columns wide, or three. Headed in thirty-six-point, boldface, extended, 'To Mr. Knapp.' Then in twelve-point: 'The woman whose property is in your possession has engaged my services (period). She is now in my office (period). She has not told me what you said to her on the phone Monday afternoon (comma), and she will not tell me (period). I know nothing of the instructions you gave her (comma), and I do not expect or care to know (period). She has hired me for a specific job (comma), to make sure that her property is returned to her in good condition (comma), and that is the purpose of this notice (paragraph).

" 'For she has hired me for another job should it become necessary (period). If her property is not returned to her (comma), or if it is damaged beyond repair (comma), I have engaged to devote my time (comma), energy (comma), and talent (comma), for as long as may be required (comma), to ensure just and fitting requital (semicolon); and she has determined to support me to the full extent of her resources (period). If you do not know enough of me to be aware of the significance of this engagement to your future (comma), I advise you to inform yourself regarding my competence and my tenacity (period).' Beneath, in fourteen-point boldface, 'Nero Wolfe.' To be billed to me. Can you do it by phone?"

"To Lon Cohen at the *Gazette,* yes. The others, maybe." I swiveled and reached for the phone, but he stopped me.

"Just a moment." He turned to Mrs. Vail. "You heard that. As you said, your husband may already be dead. If so, I am irrevocably committed by the publication of that notice. Are you? No matter what it costs in time and money?"

"Certainly. If they kill him—certainly. But I don't—Is that *all* you're going to do, just that?"

"I may not do it, madam, and if I don't I shall do nothing. There's nothing else I *could* do. I'll proceed if, and after, you give me another check for fifty thousand dollars and phone your secretary to come here at once." He slapped the chair arm. "Do you realize that I will be staking my repute, whatever credit I have established in all my years? That's what you must pay for; and the commitment. If your husband is already dead, or if Mr. Knapp, not seeing my notice or ignoring it, kills him after he gets the money, I shall have no alternative; and what if you default? I might have to spend much more than sixty thousand dollars. Of course if your husband returns safely there will be no commitment and I'll return some of it to you. How much will be in my discretion. Less if I learn that my notice was a factor; more if it wasn't. I value my reputation, which I am risking in your interest, but I am not rapacious." He looked up at the wall clock. "If what Mr. Knapp told you to do is to be done tonight, the notice must appear today to have any effect. It's nearly one o'clock."

The poor woman—or rather, the rich woman—had her teeth clamped on her lip. She looked at me. People often do that when they are being bumped around by Wolfe, apparently hoping I will come and pat them. Sometimes I wouldn't mind obliging them, but not Althea Vail, Mrs. Jimmy Vail. She just didn't warm me. Meeting her eyes, I let mine be interested but strictly professional, and when she saw that was all I had to offer she left me. She got out her checkfold, put it on the stand, and wrote, her teeth still clamping her lip. When she tore it out I was there to take it and hand it to Wolfe. Fifty grand. Wolfe gave it a glance, dropped it on his desk, and spoke.

"I hope you'll get a large part of it back, madam. I do indeed. You may use Mr. Goodwin's phone to call your secretary. When that's done he'll use it to place that notice, in all three papers if possible."

She fluttered a hand. "Is it really necessary, Mr. Wolfe? My secretary?"

"Yes, if you want me to proceed. You're going to your bank, and it will soon be lunchtime. Tell her to be here at three o'clock."

She got up and went to my chair, sat, and dialed.

2

When Dinah Utley arrived at 3:05, five minutes late, Wolfe was at his desk with a book, *The Lotus and the Robot,* by Arthur Koestler. We had started lunch later than usual because Wolfe had told Fritz not to put the shad roe in the skillet until he was notified, and it was close to half past one when I finally quit trying to persuade the *Post* and *World-Telegram* to get the ad in. Nothing doing. It was all set for the *Gazette,* thanks to Lon Cohen, who knew from experience that he would get a tit for his tat if and when. It was also set for all editions of the morning papers. The bulldogs would be out around eleven, and if Mr. Knapp saw one after he got the money and before he erased Jimmy Vail, he might change the script.

Our client had left, headed for her bank, as soon as it was definite from Lon Cohen that the ad would be in the last two editions. Part of the time while I was phoning, for some minutes at the end, Wolfe was standing at my elbow, but not to listen to me. He had the note Mrs. Vail had got from Mr. Knapp in his hand, and he pulled my typewriter around and studied the keyboard, then looked at the note, then back at the keyboard; and he kept that up, back and forth, until Fritz came to announce lunch. That was no time for me to comment or ask a question, with sautéed shad roe fresh and hot from the skillet, and the sauce, with chives and chervil and shallots, ready to be poured on, and of course nothing relating to business is ever mentioned at the table, so I waited until we had left the dining room and crossed the hall back to the office to say, "That note was typed on an Underwood, but not mine, if that's what you were checking. The 'a' is a little off-line. Also it wasn't written by me. Whoever typed it has a very uneven touch."

Sitting, he picked up *The Lotus and the Robot*. His current book is always on his desk, at the right edge of the pad, in front of the vase of orchids. That day's orchids were a raceme of Miltonia vexillaria, brought by him as usual when he had come down from the plant rooms at eleven o'clock. "Ummmp," he said. "I was merely testing a conjecture."

"Any good?"

"Yes." He opened the book to his place and swiveled, giving me his acre or so of back. If I wanted to test a conjecture I would have to use one of my own. A visitor was due in ten minutes, and since according to him the best digestive-is a book because it occupies the mind and leaves the stomach in privacy, he darned well was going to get a few pages in. And when, a quarter of an hour later, I having spent most of it inspecting the note from Mr. Knapp with occasional glances at my typewriter keyboard, the doorbell rang, and I went to the hall and returned with the visitor, and pronounced her name, and put her in the red leather chair, Wolfe stuck with his book until I had gone to my desk and sat. Then he marked his place and put it down, looked at her, and said, "Are you an efficient secretary, Miss Utley?"

Her eyes widened a little, and she smiled. If she had been doing any crying along with her employer it had certainly left no traces. At sight I had guessed her age at thirty, but that might have been a couple of years short.

"I earn my salary, Mr. Wolfe," she said.

She was cool—cool eyes, cool smile, cool voice. With some cool ones the reaction is that it would be interesting to apply a little heat and see what happens, and you wouldn't mind trying, but with others you feel that they are cool clear through, and she was one of them, though there was nothing wrong with her features or figure. You could even call her a looker.

Wolfe was taking her in. "No doubt," he said. "As you know, Mrs. Vail phoned you from here. I heard her tell you not to tell me what Mr. Knapp said to her on the phone yesterday, but you may feel that she is under great

strain and your judgment on that point is better than
hers. Do you?"

"No." Very cool. "I'm in her employ."

"Then I won't try to cajole you. Do you always open
Mrs. Vail's mail?"

"Yes."

"Everything that comes?"

"Yes."

"How many items were there in yesterday morning's
mail?"

"I didn't count them. Perhaps twenty."

"The envelope with that note in it, did you open it first
or further along in the process?"

Of course that tactic is three thousand years old,
maybe more, asking for a detail of a reported action,
looking for hesitation or confusion. Dinah Utley smiled.
"I always sort it out first, leaving circulars and other obvious stuff until later. Yesterday there were four—no, five
—that I opened at once. The envelope with that note was
the third one I opened."

"Did you show it to Mrs. Vail at once?"

"Certainly. I took it to her room."

"Were you present Sunday night when she phoned to
the country to ask about her husband?"

"No. I was in the house, but I was in bed."

"What time yesterday did the call come from Mr.
Knapp?"

"Eight minutes after four. I knew that might be important somehow, and I made a note of it."

"You listened to that conversation?"

"Yes. Mrs. Vail had told me to take it down, and I
did."

"Then you know shorthand?"

"Of course."

"Are you a college graduate?"

"Yes."

"Do you type with two fingers, or four?"

She smiled. "All of them. By touch." She turned a
hand over. "Really, Mr. Wolfe. Isn't this rather silly? Is it
going to get Mr. Vail back alive?"

"No. But it may conceivably serve a purpose. Naturally you want to be with Mrs. Vail, and she wants you; I

won't keep you much longer. There's no point now in
asking you about that man's voice and diction; even if I
got a hint that suggested another wording for the notice
it's too late. But you will please let Mr. Goodwin take
samples of your fingerprints. Archie?"

That roused her a little. *"My* fingerprints? Why?"

"Not to get Mr. Vail back alive. But they may be useful later on. It's barely possible that Mr. Knapp or an accomplice inadvertently left a print on that note. To your
knowledge, has anyone handled it besides Mrs. Vail and
you?"

"No."

"And Mr. Goodwin and me. We shall get Mrs. Vail's.
Mr. Goodwin is an expert on prints, and even if Mr. Vail
returns safely, as I hope he will, we'll want to know if
there are any unidentifiable prints on that note. Do you
object to having your prints taken?

"Of course not. Why should I?"

"Then Archie?"

I had opened a desk drawer and was getting out the
equipment—ink with dauber and surfaced paper. I prefer
a dauber to a pad. Knowing now, as I did, what the conjecture was that Wolfe had been testing when he inspected my typewriter keyboard with the note from Mr.
Knapp in his hand, and therefore also knowing why I was
to take Dinah Utley's prints, it wasn't necessary to write
her name on the paper, but I did anyway. She got up and
came to my desk and I did her right hand first. She had
good hands, firm, smooth, well kept, with long slender fingers. No rings. With her left hand, when I had done the
thumb, index, and middle, and started to daub the ring
finger, I asked casually, "What's this? Scald it?"

"No. Shut a drawer on it."

"The pinkie too. I'll go easy."

"It's not very tender now. I did it several days ago."

But I went easy, there being no point in making her
suffer, since we had no use for the prints. As she cleaned
her fingers with solvent and tissues she asked Wolfe,
"You don't really think a kidnaper would be fool enough
to leave his fingerprint on that note, do you?"

"No," Wolfe said, "not fool enough. But possibly dis-
traught enough. One thing more, Miss Utley. I would like

you to know that I'm aware that the primary concern is
the safety of Mr. Vail. I have done all I can. Archie,
show her a copy of the notice.

I got it from my desk and handed it to her. Wolfe
waited until she had finished reading it to say, "That will
appear, prominently, in today's *Gazette* and the morning
papers. If the kidnaper sees it, it may have an effect; it
certainly will if he has some knowledge of me. For I will
have publicly committed myself, and if he kills Mr. Vail
he will be doomed inevitably. A month, a year, ten years;
no matter. It's regrettable that you or I can't reach him,
to make that clear to him."

"Yes, it is." Still perfectly cool. She handed me the notice. "Of course he may not have as high an opinion of
your abilities as you have." She turned to go, after three
steps stopped and turned her head to say, "He might even
think the police are more dangerous than you are," and
went. There ahead of her, and preceding her to the hall
and the front door, I let her out; and, expecting no
thanks or good day, got none.

Returning to the office, I stopped in front of Wolfe's
desk, stood looking down at him, and said, "So she typed
it."

He nodded. "Of course I didn't—"

"Excuse me. I'll do the spiel. When you first looked at
it you noticed, as I did, that whoever typed it had an uneven touch. Later, while I was phoning, you looked at it
again, got an idea, and came and compared it with the
keyboard, and you saw that all the letters that were faint
were on the left—not just left of center, but at the left
end. W, E, A, S, and D. So you conjectured that the typist had been someone who used all his fingers, not just
two or four, and that for some—"

"And probably typed by touch, because—"

"Excuse me, I'm doing the spiel. The touch was merely
a probable. And for some reason the ring and little fingers of his left hand had not hit the keys as hard as the
other fingers, not nearly as hard. Okay. I caught up with
you after lunch, while you were reading, just before she
came. You saw me comparing the note with the keyboard."

"No. I was reading."

"Let me not believe that. You miss nothing, though you often pretend to. You saw me all right. Then she came, and you went on ahead of me again, and I admit I ought to be docked. My eyes are as good as yours, and I had been closer to her than you were, but you noticed that the tips of those two fingers on her left hand were discolored and slightly swollen, and I didn't. Of course when you told her we wanted her prints I saw it, and you will ignore what I said about being docked because I found out how and when the fingers got hurt. Any corrections?"

"No. It is still a conjecture, not a conclusion."

"Damn close to it. One will get you fifty. That it is just a coincidence that she, a touch typist, living in that house, hurt just those two fingers, just at that time, just enough to make her go easy with them but not enough to stop using them—nuts. One will get you a hundred. So you had her read that notice and rubbed it in, thinking she'll get in touch with Mr. Knapp. Why did you let her walk out?"

Wolfe nodded. "The alternative was obvious. Go at her. Would she have yielded?"

"No. She's tough."

"And if Mr. Vail is already dead, as he well may be, it would be folly to let her know what we suspect. If he is alive, no better. She would have flouted me. Detain her forcibly, as a hostage, on a mere suspicion, however well grounded, and notify Mr. Knapp that we would exchange her for Mr. Vail? That would have been a coup, but how to reach Mr. Knapp? It's too late to get another notice in the paper. Have you a suggestion?"

"Yes. I go to see Mrs. Vail to ask her something, no matter what, and I manage somehow to get something written on the typewriter Dinah Utley uses. Of course she could have used another machine for the note, but if what I got matched the note, that would settle that."

He shook his head. "No. You have ingenuity and can even be delicate, but Miss Utley would almost certainly get a hint. Besides, to ask a question she asked, would it help to get Mr. Vail back alive? No." He glanced at the clock. In ten minutes he would leave for his four-to-six afternoon session in the plant rooms. Time enough for a few pages. He reached and got his book and opened to his place.

3

It's possible that I have given a wrong impression of Jimmy Vail, and if so I should correct it.

Age, thirty-four; height, five feet ten; weight, 150. Dark eyes, sometimes lazy and dull, sometimes bright and very quick. Smooth dark hair, nearly black, and a neat white face with a wide mouth. I had seen him about as often as I had seen his wife, since they were nearly always together at a restaurant or theater. In 1956 he had made a big splash at the Glory Hole in the Village with a thirty-minute turn of personal chatter, pointed comments on everyone and everything. Althea Tedder, widow of Harold F. Tedder, had seen him there, and in 1957 she had married him, or he had married her, depending on who is talking.

I suppose any woman who marries a man a dozen years younger is sure to get the short end of the stick when her name comes up among friends, let alone enemies, no matter what the facts are. The talk may have been just talk. Women of any age liked Jimmy Vail and liked to be with him, there was no question about that, and undoubtedly he could have two-timed his middle-aged wife any day in the week if he felt like it, but I had never with my own eyes seen him in the act. I'm merely saying that as far as I know, disregarding talk, he was a model husband. I had expected her to ask Wolfe to put a tail on him because I assumed that her friends had seen to it that she knew about the talk.

She also had made a public splash, twenty-five years back—Althea Purcell as the milkmaid in *Meadow Lark* —and she had quit to marry a man somewhat older and a lot richer. They had produced two children, a son and daughter; I had seen them a couple of times at the Flamingo. Tedder had died in 1954, so Althea had waited a decent interval to get a replacement.

Actually, neither Jimmy nor Althea had done anything notorious, or even conspicuous, during the four years of their marriage. They were mentioned frequently in print only because they were expected to do something any minute. She had left Broadway in the middle of a smash hit to marry a middle-aged rich man with a prominent name, and he had left the mike in the middle of *his* smash hit to marry a middle-aged rich woman. With the Tedder house and the Tedder dough taken over by a pair like that, anything might happen and probably would. That was the idea.

Now something *had* happened, something sensational, two days ago, and not a word about it in print. There was nothing in Nero Wolfe's notice to Mr. Knapp to connect it with the Vails. If Helen Blount, Mrs. Vail's friend, saw it, she might make a guess, but not for publication. I saw it not long after Wolfe went up to the plant rooms. Not waiting until five-thirty when a late edition of the *Gazette* is delivered to the old brownstone, I took a walk to the newsstand at 34th and Eighth Avenue. It was on page five, with plenty of margin. No one named Knapp could possibly miss it, but of course that wasn't his name.

I had a date for that evening, dinner with a friend, and a show, and it was just as well. Most of the chores of a working detective, even Nero Wolfe's right hand, not to mention his legs, are routine and pretty damn dull, and the idea of tailing a woman taking half a million bucks to a kidnaper was very tempting. Not only would it have been an interesting way to spend an evening, but there were a dozen possibilities. But since it was Wolfe's case and I was working for him, I couldn't do it without his knowledge and consent, and it would have been a waste of breath to mention it. He would have said pfui and picked up his book. So at six o'clock I went up to my room and changed and went to my date. But off and on that evening I wondered where our client was and how she was making out, and when I got home around one o'clock I had a job keeping myself from dialing her number before I turned in.

The phone rang. Of all the things that I don't want to be wakened by, the one I resent most is the phone. I turned over, forced my eyes open enough to see that it was light and the clock said 7:52, reached for the receiver and got it to my ear, and managed to get it out: "Nero Wolfe's residence, Archie Goodwin speaking."

"Mr. Goodwin?"

"I thought I said so."

"This is Althea Vail. I want to speak to Mr. Wolfe."

"Impossible, Mrs. Vail. Not before breakfast. If it's urgent, tell me. Have you—"

"My husband is back! Safe and sound!"

"Good. Wonderful. Is he there with you?"

"No, he's at our country place. He just phoned, ten minutes ago. He's going to bathe and change and eat and then come to town. He's all right, perfectly all right. Why I'm phoning, he promised them he would say nothing, absolutely nothing, for forty-eight hours, and I'm not to say anything either. I didn't tell him I had gone to Nero Wolfe; I'll wait till he gets here. Of course I don't want Mr. Wolfe to say anything. Or you. That's why I'm phoning. You'll tell him?"

"Yes. With pleasure. You're sure it was your husband on the phone?"

"Certainly I'm sure!"

"Fine. Whether the notice helped or not. Will you give us a ring when your husband arrives?"

She said she would, and we hung up. The radio clicked on, and a voice came: ". . . has five convenient offices in New York, one at the—" I reached and turned it off. When I get to bed after midnight I set it for eight o'clock, the news bulletins on WQXR, but I didn't need any more news at the moment. I had a satisfactory stretch and yawn, said aloud, "What the hell, no matter what Jimmy Vail says we can say Mr. Knapp *must* have seen it," yawned again, and faced the fact that it takes will power to get on your feet.

With nothing pending I took my time, and it was after eight-thirty when I descended the two flights to the ground floor, entered the kitchen, told Fritz good morning, picked up my glass of orange juice, took a healthy sip, and felt my stomach saying thanks. I had considered stopping at Wolfe's room on the way down but had vetoed it. He would have been in the middle of breakfast, since Fritz takes his tray up at eight-fifteen.

"No allspice in the sausage," Fritz said. "It would be an insult. The best Mr. Howie has ever sent us."

"Then double my order." I swallowed juice. "You gave me good news, so I'll give you some. The woman that came yesterday gave us a job, and it's already done. All over. Enough to pay your salary and mine for months."

"*Fort bien.*" He spooned batter on the griddle. "You did it last night?"

"No. He did it sitting down."

"Yes? But he would do nothing without you to *piquer.*"

"How do you spell that?"

He spelled it. I said, "I'll look it up," put my empty glass down, went to the table against the wall where my copy of the *Times* was on the rack, and sat. I kept an eye on my watch, and at 8:57, when I had downed the last bite of my first griddle cake and my second sausage, I reached for the house phone and buzzed Wolfe's room.

His growl came. "Yes?"

"Good morning. Mrs. Vail called an hour ago. Her husband had just phoned from their house in the country. He's at large and intact and will come to town as soon as he cleans up and feeds. He promised someone, presumably Mr. Knapp, that neither he nor his wife will make a peep for forty-eight hours, and she wants us to keep the lid on."

"Satisfactory."

"Yeah. Nice and neat. But I'll be taking a walk, to the bank to deposit her checks, and it's only five more blocks to the *Gazette.* It's bound to break soon, and I could give it to Lon Cohen to hold until we give the word. He'd hold it, you know that, and he would deeply appreciate it."

"No."

"You mean he wouldn't hold it?"

"No. He has shown that he can be trusted. But I haven't seen Mr. Vail, nor have you. It's useful to have Mr. Cohen in our debt, but no. Perhaps later in the day."

He hung up. He would be two minutes late getting to the plant rooms on the roof. As Fritz brought my second cake and pair of sausages I said, "For a bent nickel I'd go up and peekay him."

He patted my shoulder and said, "Now, Archie. If you should, you will. If you shouldn't, you won't."

I buttered the cake. "I *think* that's a compliment. It's tricky. I'll study it."

For the next couple of hours, finishing breakfast and the *Times* (the notice was on page twenty-six), opening the mail, dusting our desks, removing yesterday's orchids and putting fresh water in the vase, walking to the bank and back, and doing little miscellaneous office chores, I considered the situation off and on. It seemed pretty damn silly, being hired in connection with something as gaudy as the kidnaping of Jimmy Vail, merely to put a ad in the paper and collect a fee and then call it a day. But what else? I'm more than willing to peekay Wolfe when there's any point or profit to it, but with Jimmy Vail back in one piece the job Wolfe had been hired for was done, so what? As soon as it broke, an army of cops and FBI scientists would be after Mr. Knapp, and they'd probably get him sooner or later. We were done, except for one little detail, to see Jimmy Vail whole. Mrs. Vail had said she would give us a ring when he arrived, and I would go up and ask him if Mr. Knapp had shown him the *Gazette* with the notice in it.

I didn't have to. At 11:25 the doorbell rang. Wolfe had come down from the plant rooms and gone to his desk, put a spray of Oncidium marshallianum in the vase, torn yesterday from his desk calendar, and gone through the mail, and was dictating a long letter to an orchid collector in Guatemala. He hates to be interrupted when he's doing something really important, but Fritz was upstairs, so I went, and there he was on the stoop. I told Wolfe, "Jimmy Vail in person," and went and opened the door, and he said, "Maybe you know me? I know you." He stepped in. "You're a hell of a good dancer."

I told him he was too, which was true, took his coat and hat and put them on the rack, and took him to the office, and he crossed to Wolfe's desk, stood, and said, "I know you don't shake hands. I once offered to fight a man because he called you a panjandrum; of course I knew he was yellow. I'm Jimmy Vail. May I sit down? Preferably in the red leather chair. There it is." He went and sat, rested his elbows on the chair arms, crossed his legs, and said, "If I belch you'll have to pardon me. I had nothing but cold canned beans for two days and three nights, and I overdid it on the bacon and eggs. My wife has told me about hiring you. Never has so much been spent on so little. Naturally I don't like being called my wife's property—who would?—but I realize you had to. I only saw it when my wife showed it to me, and I don't know whether they saw it or not. Is that important?"

You wouldn't have thought, looking at him and listening to him, that he had just spent sixty hours in the clutches of kidnapers, living on cold beans, and maybe not long to live even on beans, but of course he had cleaned up and had a meal, and the talk I had heard had never included any suggestion that he was a softy. His face was dead white, but it always was, and smooth and neat as it always was, and his dark eyes were bright and clear.

"It would be helpful to know," Wolfe said, "but it isn't vital. You came to tell me that? That you don't know?"

"Not actually." Vail lifted a hand to the neighborhood of his right temple and flipped his middle finger off the tip of his thumb. He had made that gesture famous during his career at the Glory Hole. "I just mentioned it because it may be important to us, my wife and me. If one of them saw that thing in the paper they know my wife has told you about it, and that may not be too good. That's why I came and came quick. They told me to keep my trap shut for forty-eight hours, until Friday morning, and to see that my wife did too, or we would regret it. I think they meant it. I got a strong impression that they mean what they say. So my wife and I are going to keep it to ourselves until Friday morning, but what about you? You could put another notice in the paper to Mr. Knapp, saying that since the property has been returned the case is closed as far as you're concerned. That you're no longer interested. What do you think?"

Wolfe had cocked his head and was eying him. "You're making an unwarranted assumption, Mr. Vail—that I too will keep silent until Friday morning. I told your wife that the obligation not to withhold knowledge of a major crime must sometimes bow to other considerations, for instance saving a life, but you are no longer in jeopardy. Now that I've seen you alive and at freedom, I cannot further postpone reporting to authority. A licensed private detective is under constraints that do not apply to the ordinary citizen. I don't want to subject you or your wife—"

The phone rang, and I swiveled to get it. "Nero Wolfe's office, Archie Good—"

"This is Althea Vail. Is my husband there?"

"Yes, he—"

"I want to speak to him."

She sounded urgent. I proceeded as I did not merely out of curiosity. There was obviously going to be a collision between Wolfe and Jimmy Vail about saving it until Friday, and if that was what she was urgent about I wanted to hear it firsthand. So I told her to hold the wire, told him his wife wanted to speak to him, and beat it, to the kitchen and the extension there. As I got the receiver to my ear Mrs. Vail was talking.

". . . terrible has happened. A man just phoned from White Plains, Captain Saunders of the State Police, he said, and he said they found a dead body, a woman, and it's Dinah Utley, they think it is, and they want me to come to White Plains to identify it or send someone. My God, Jimmy, *could* it be Dinah? How could it be Dinah?"

JIMMY: I don't know. Maybe Archie Goodwin will know; he's listening in on an extension. Did he say how she was killed?

ALTHEA: No. He—

JIMMY: Or where the body was found?

ALTHEA: No. He—

JIMMY: Or why they think it's Dinah Utley?

ALTHEA: Yes, things in her bag and in the car. Her car was there. I don't think—I don't want to—can't I send Emil?

JIMMY: Why not? How about it, Goodwin? Emil is the chauffeur. He can certainly tell them whether it's Dinah Utley or not. Must my wife go? Or must I go?

It was no use pretending I wasn't there. "No," I said, "not just for identification. Of course if it's Dinah Utley they'll want to ask both of you some questions, if there's any doubt about how she died, but for that they can come to you. For identification only, even I would do. If you want to ask Mr. Wolfe to send me."

ALTHEA: Yes! Do that, Jimmy!

JIMMY: Well . . . maybe . . . where did he say to come in White Plains?

ME: I know where to go.

ALTHEA: It must be Dinah! She didn't come home last night and now—this is terrible—

JIMMY: Take it easy, Al. I'll be there soon. Just take it easy and . . .

I cradled the phone and went back to the office. Vail was hanging up as I entered. I said to him, "Naturally I want to hear what a client of Mr. Wolfe's has to say on his phone. And naturally you knew I would." I turned to Wolfe. "A state cop called Mrs. Vail from White Plains. They have found a woman's body, he didn't say where, and from articles in her bag and her car they think it's Dinah Utley. Also there must have been something that connected her with Mrs. Vail, maybe just the address. He asked Mrs. Vail to come to White Plains and identify her, and she doesn't want to go, and neither does Mr. Vail. I suggested that she might want to ask you to send me."

Wolfe was scowling at Vail. He switched it to me. "Did she die by violence?"

"Mrs. Vail doesn't know. I've reported in full."

"Look," Vail said, "this is a hell of a thing." He was standing at the corner of my desk. "Good God. This is a real shocker. I suppose I ought to go myself."

"If it's Miss Utley," Wolfe said, "and if she died by violence, they'll ask you where you were last night. That would be routine."

"I'm not telling anyone where I was last night, not until Friday morning. Not even you."

"Then you'll be suspect. You and your wife should confer without delay. And if Mr. Goodwin goes to identify the body and it is Miss Utley, he will be asked about his association with her, when and where he has seen her. You know she was here yesterday?"

"Yes. My wife told me. But my God, he won't tell them about that, why she came here!"

Wolfe leaned back and shut his eyes. Vail started to say something, saw he wouldn't be heard, and stopped.

He went to the red leather chair and sat, then got up again, walked halfway to the door, turned, and came back to Wolfe's desk and stood looking down at him.

Wolfe's eyes opened, and he straightened up. "Archie, get Mrs. Vail."

"I'm here," Vail said. "You can talk to me."

"You're not my client, Mr. Vail. Your wife is."

I was dialing. The number was in my head, where I had filed it when I looked it up Tuesday night. A female voice said, "Mrs. Vail's residence," and I said Nero Wolfe wanted to speak with Mrs. Vail. After a wait our client's voice came, "This is Althea Vail. Mr. Wolfe?" and I nodded to Wolfe and he took his phone. I stayed on, but I had to fight for it. Jimmy Vail came to take it away from me, reaching for it and getting his fingers on it, but I kept it against my ear and didn't hear what he said because I was listening to Wolfe.

"Good morning, madam. I was gratified to see your husband, as of course you were. The telephone call you received from White Plains puts a new problem, and I offer a suggestion. I understand that you prefer not to go to White Plains to see if the dead woman is Miss Utley. Is that correct?"

"Yes. Archie Goodwin said he would go."

Wolfe grunted. "Mr. Goodwin will always go. He is uh—energetic. But there are difficulties. If it is Miss Utley, he will be asked when and where he last saw her, and when he says she came to my office yesterday he will be asked for particulars. If he gives them in full he will have to include the fact that when she left we, he and I, had formed a strong suspicion that she was implicated in the kidnaping of your husband, and then—"

"Dinah? She was implicated? That's ridiculous! Why did you suspect that?"

"I reserve that. I'll explain it later—or I won't. Then they'll demand full information about the kidnaping, not only from Mr. Goodwin and me, but from you and your husband, and they won't want to wait until Friday for it. That's the prob—"

"But why did you suspect *Dinah?*"

"That will have to wait. So I offer a suggestion. You gave me checks for sixty thousand dollars. I told you I would refund a portion of it if your husband came back alive, since it covered the contingency that I might have to meet the commitment I made in that published notice. I would prefer to keep it, but if I do I'll have to earn it. My suggestion is that I send Mr. Goodwin to White Plains to look at the body. If it is Miss Utley, he identifies it, he says that he saw her for the first and last time when she came to my office yesterday in connection with a confidential job you had hired me for, and on instructions from me he refuses to give any further information. Also I engage that neither he nor I will disclose anything whatever regarding your husband's kidnaping before eleven o'clock Friday morning unless you give your consent. That will expose us to inconvenience and possibly serious embarrassment, and I shall not feel obliged to return any money to you. I will owe you nothing, and you will owe me nothing. That's my suggestion. I should add, not to coerce you, merely to inform you, that if it isn't accepted I can no longer withhold my knowledge of a capital crime, kidnaping. I'll have to inform the proper authority immediately."

"That's a threat. That's blackmail."

"Pfui. I've offered to incur a considerable risk for a moderate fee. I withdraw my suggestion. I'll send you a check today. That will end—"

"No! Don't hang up!" Nothing for five seconds. "I want to speak to my husband."

"Very well." Wolfe looked around, then at me, and demanded, "Where is he?"

I covered the transmitter. "Skipped. Right after you said we suspected that Dinah was implicated. Gone. I heard the front door close."

"I didn't." He returned to the phone. "Your husband has left, Mrs. Vail, presumably to go to you. I didn't see him go. I'll send you a check—"

"No!" Another silence, a little longer. "All right, send Archie Goodwin. To White Plains."

"With the understanding that I proposed?"

"Yes. But I want to know why you thought Dinah was implicated. That's incredible!"

"To you, no doubt. It was merely a conjecture, possibly ill-grounded. Another time I may explain it, but not now. I must get Mr. Goodwin off. Permit me."

He hung up, and so did I. I got up and crossed to the hall, went to the front door to see that it was closed, opened the door to the front room and looked in, returned to the office, and told Wolfe, "He's gone. Not that I thought our client's husband would try any tricks, but he might have got confused and shut the door while he was still inside. Instructions?"

"Not necessary. You heard what I said to Mrs. Vail."

"Yeah, that's okay, the worst they can do is toss me in the jug, and what the hell, you're getting paid for it. But are we curious about anything? Do we care what happened to her, and when and where?"

"No. We are not concerned."

I headed for the hall, but at the door I turned. "You know," I said, "some day it may cost you something. You know damned well that we may have to be concerned and you may have to work, and it might be helpful for me to collect a few facts while they're still warm. But will you admit it? No. Why? Because you think I'm so—uh —energetic that I'll get the facts anyhow and have them available if and when you need them. For once I won't. If somebody wants to tell me no matter what, I'll say I'm not concerned."

I went and got my coat from the rack, no hat, let myself out, descended the seven steps to the sidewalk, walked to Tenth Avenue and around the corner to the garage, and got the 1961 Heron sedan which Wolfe owns and I drive.

4

At one-fifteen p.m. Clark Hobart, District Attorney of Westchester County, narrowed his eyes at me and said, "You're dry behind the ears, Goodwin. You know what you're letting yourself in for."

We were in his office at the Court House, a big corner room with four windows. He was seated at his desk, every inch an elected servant of the people. With a strong jaw, a keen eye, and big ears that stuck out. My chair was at an end of the desk. In two chairs in front of it were Captain Saunders of the State Police and a man I had had contacts with before, Ben Dykes, head of the county detectives. Dykes had fattened some in the two years since I had last seen him; what had been a crease was now a gully, giving him two chins, and when he sat his belly lapped over his belt. But the word was that he was still a fairly smart cop.

I met Hobart's eyes, straight but not belligerent. "I'd like to be sure," I said, "that you've got it right. They reported to you before I was brought in. I don't suppose they twisted it deliberately, I know Ben Dykes wouldn't, but let's avoid any misunderstanding. I looked at the corpse and identified it as Dinah Utley. Captain Saunders asked me how well I had known her, and I said I had met her only once, yesterday afternoon, but my identification was positive. Dykes asked where I had met her yesterday afternoon, and I said at Nero Wolfe's office. He asked what she was there for, and I said Mrs. Jimmy Vail had told her to come, at Mr. Wolfe's request, so he could ask her some questions in connection with a confidential matter which Mrs. Vail had hired him to investigate. He asked me what the confidential matter was, and I—"

"And you refused to tell him."

I nodded. "That's the point. My refusal was qualified. I said I was under instructions from Mr. Wolfe. If he would tell me where the body had been found, and how and when and where she had died, with details, I would report to Mr. Wolfe, and if a crime had been committed he would decide whether it was reasonable to suppose that the crime was in any way connected with the matter Mrs. Vail had consulted him about. I hadn't quite finished when Captain Saunders broke in and said Dinah Utley had been murdered and I damned well would tell him then and there exactly what she had said to Mr. Wolfe and what he had said to her. I said I damned well wouldn't, and he said he had heard how tough I thought I was and he would take me where we wouldn't be disturbed and find out. Evidently he's the salt-of-the-earth type. Ben Dykes, who is just a cop, no hero, insisted on bringing me to you. If what I'm letting myself in for is being turned over to Captain Saunders, that would suit me fine. I have been thinking of going to a psychiatrist to find out how tough I am, and that would save me the trouble."

"I'll be glad to do you that favor," Saunders said. He moved his lips the minimum required to get the words out. Someone had probably told him that that showed you had power in reserve, and he had practiced it before a mirror.

"You're not being turned over," Hobart said. "I'm the chief law officer of this county. A crime *has* been committed. Dinah Utley was murdered. She was with you not many hours before she died, and as far as we know now, you were the last person to see her alive. Captain Saunders was fully justified in asking for the details of that interview. So am I."

I shook my head. "He didn't ask, he demanded. As for the crime, where and when? If a car ran over her this—"

"How do you know a car ran over her?" Saunders snapped.

I ignored him. "If a car ran over her this morning here on Main Street, and people who saw the driver say he was a dwarf with whiskers and one eye, I doubt if Mr. Wolfe will think his talk with her yesterday was relevant. Having seen the body, I assume that either a car ran over her or she was hit several times with a sledgehammer though there are other possibilities." I turned a hand over. "What the hell, Mr. Hobart. You know Mr. Wolfe knows the rules."

He nodded. "And I know how he abuses them—and you too. Dinah Utley wasn't killed here on Main Street. Her body was found at ten o'clock this morning by two boys who should have been in school. It was in a ditch by a roadside, where it—"

"What road?"

"Iron Mine Road. Presumably it once led to an iron mine, but now it leads nowhere. It's narrow and rough, and it come to a dead end about two miles from Route One Twenty-three. The body—"

"Where does it leave Route One Twenty-three?"

Saunders growled, in his throat, not parting his lips. He got ignored again.

"About two miles from where Route One Twenty-three

leaves Route Thirty-five," Hobart said. "South of Ridge-field, not far from the state line. The body had been rolled into the ditch after death. The car that had run over her was there, about a hundred feet away up the road, headed into an opening to the woods. The registration for the car was in it, with the name Dinah Utley and the address Nine Ninety-four Fifth Avenue, New York twenty-eight. Also in it was her handbag, containing the usual items, some of them bearing her name. It has been established that it was that car that ran over her. Anything else?"

"When did she die?"

"Oh, of course. The limits are nine o'clock last evening and three o'clock this morning."

"Were there traces of another car?"

"Yes. One and possibly two, but on grass. The road's gravelly, and the grass is thick up to the gravel."

"Anyone who saw Dinah Utley or her car last night, or another car?"

"Not so far. The nearest house is nearly half a mile away, east, toward Route One Twenty-three, and that stretch of road is seldom traveled."

"Have you got any kind of a lead?"

"Yes. You. When a woman is murdered a few hours after she goes to see a private detective it's a fair assumption that the two events were connected and what she said to the detective is material. Were you present when she talked with Wolfe?"

"Yes. It's also a fair assumption that the detective is the best judge as to whether the two events were connected or not. As I said Dinah Utley didn't come to see Mr. Wolfe on her own hook; she came because Mrs. Vail told her to, to give him some information about something Mrs. Vail wanted done." I got up. "Okay, you've told me what I can read in the paper in a couple of hours. I'll report to Mr. Wolfe and give you a ring."

"That's what you think." Saunders was on his feet. "Mr. Hobart, you know how important time is on a thing like this. You realize that if you let him go in twenty minutes he'll be out of your jurisdiction. You realize that he has information that if we get it now it might make all the difference."

I grinned at him. "Can you do twenty pushups? I can."

Ben Dykes told Hobart, "I'd like to ask him something," and Hobart told him to go ahead. Dykes turned to me. "There was an ad in the *Gazette* yesterday headed 'to Mr. Knapp' with Nero Wolfe's name at the bottom. Did that have anything to do with why Mrs. Vail told Dinah Utley to go to see Wolfe?"

The word that Dykes was still a fairly smart cop seemed to be based on facts. The grin I gave him was not the one I had given Saunders. "Sorry," I said, "but I'm under orders from the man I work for." I went to the District Attorney. "You know the score, Mr. Hobart. It would be stretching a point even to hold me for questioning as it stands now, and since I wouldn't answer the questions, and since Mr. Wolfe wouldn't talk on the phone or let anyone in the house until he gets my report, I suppose we'll have to let Captain Saunders go without. But of course it's your murder."

He had his head tilted back to frown at me. "You know the penalty," he said, "for obstructing justice." When I said, "Yes, sir," politely, he abruptly doubled his fists, bounced up out of his chair, and yelled, "Get the hell out of here!" As I turned to obey, Ben Dykes shook his head at me. I passed close enough to Saunders for him to stick out a foot and trip me, but he didn't.

Down on the sidewalk, I looked at my watch: 1:35. I walked three blocks to a place I knew about, called Mary Jane's, where someone makes chicken pie the way my Aunt Anna used to make it in Chillicothe, Ohio, with fluffy little dumplings; and as I went through a dish of it I considered the situation. There was no point in wasting money ringing Wolfe, since he wasn't concerned, and as for our client, there was no rush. I could call her after I reported to Wolfe. So, since I was already halfway there —well, a third of the way—why not take a look at Iron Mine Road? And maybe at the old iron mine if I could find it? If I kidnaped a man and wanted a place to keep him while I collected half a million bucks, I wouldn't ask anything better than an abandoned iron mine. I paid for the chicken and a piece of rhubarb pie, walked to the lot where I had parked the Heron, ransomed it, and headed for Hawthorne Circle. There I took the Saw Mill River

Parkway, and at its end, at Katonah, I took Route 35 east. It was a bright sunny day, and I fully appreciate things like forsythia and trees starting to bud and cows in pastures as long as I have a car that I can depend on to get me back to town. Just short of Connecticut I turned right onto Route 123, glancing at my speedometer. When I had gone a mile and a half I started looking for Iron Mine Road, and in another two-tenths there it was.

After negotiating a mile of that road I wasn't so sure that the Heron would get me back to town. I met five cars in the mile, and for one of them I had to climb a bank and for another I had to back up fifty yards. There was no problem about spotting the scene of the crime when I finally reached it. There were eight cars strung along, blocking the road completely, none of them official. A dozen women and three or four men were standing at the roadside, at the edge of the ditch, and two men at the other side of the road were having a loud argument about who had dented whose fender. I didn't even bother to get out. To the north was thick woods, and to the south a steep rocky slope with a swamp at the bottom. I admit I was a little vague about what an abandoned iron mine should look like, but nothing in sight looked promising. I pushed the reverse button and started backing, with care, and eventually came to a spot with enough room to turn around. On the way to Route 123 I met three cars coming in.

Of the two decisions I made going back to town, I was aware of one of them at the time I made it, which was par. That one was to take my time, with half an eye on the landscape, to see how the country was making out with its spring chores, which was sensible, since I couldn't get to 35th Street before four o'clock and Wolfe would be up in the plant rooms, where he hates to be interrupted, especially when there's nothing stirring that he's concerned about. I made that decision before I reached Route 35.

I don't know when the other decision was made. I became aware of it when I found myself in the middle lane of the Thruway, hitting sixty-five. When I'm bound for New York from Westchester and my destination is on the West Side, I take the Saw Mill all the way; when my destination is on the East Side I leave it at Ardsley and get on the Thruway. And there I was on the Thruway, so obviously I was going somewhere on the East Side. Where? It took me nearly two seconds. I'll be damned, I told myself, I'm headed for our client's house to tell her I identified the body. Okay, that will save a dime, the cost of a phone call. And if her husband is there and they have any questions, I can answer them face to face, which is always more satisfactory. I rolled on, to the Major Deegan Expressway, the East River Drive, and the 96th Street exit.

It was ten minutes past four when, having found a space on 81st Street I could squeeze the Heron into, I entered the vestibule of the four-story stone mansion at 994 Fifth Avenue and pushed the button. The door was opened by a square-faced woman in uniform with a smudge on her cheek. I suppose the Tedder who had had the house built, Harold F.'s father, wouldn't have dreamed of letting that door be opened by a female, so it was just as well he wasn't around. She had a surprise for me, though she didn't know it. When I gave my name and I said I wanted to see Mrs. Vail, she said Mrs. Vail was expecting me, and made room for me to enter. I shouldn't have been surprised to find once again that Wolfe thought he knew me as well as I thought I knew him, but I was. What had happened, of course, was that Mrs. Vail had phoned to ask if I had identified the body, and he had told her that I would stop at her house on the way back from White Plains, though that hadn't been mentioned by him or me. That was how well he thought he knew me. Some day he'll overdo it. As I have said, *I* hadn't known I was going to stop at her house until I found myself on the Thruway.

As the female door-opener took my coat, a tenor voice came from above, "Who is it, Elga?" and Elga answered it, "It's Mr. Goodwin, Mr. Tedder," and the tenor called, "Come on up, Mr. Goodwin." I went and mounted the marble stairs, white, wide, and winding, and at the top there was Noel Tedder. I've mentioned that I had seen him a few times, but I had never met him. From hearsay he was a twenty-three-year-old brat who had had a try at three colleges but couldn't make it, who had been forced by his mother to stop climbing mountains because he had fallen off of one, and who had once landed a helicopter on second base at Yankee Stadium in the fifth inning of a ball game; but from my personal knowledge he was merely a broad-shouldered six-footer who didn't care how he dressed when he went to the theater or the Flamingo and who talked too loud after two drinks. The tenor voice was one of those mistakes that get made when the hands are being dealt.

He took me down a wide hall to an open door and motioned me in. I crossed the sill and stopped, thinking for a second I had crashed a party, but then I saw that only five of the people in the room were alive, the rest were bronze or stone, and I remembered a picture I had seen years ago of Harold F. Tedder's library. This was it. It was a big room, high-ceilinged, but it looked a little crowded with a dozen life-sized statues standing around here and there. If he liked company he sure had it. Mrs. Vail's voice came, "Over here, Mr. Goodwin," and I moved. The five live ones were in a group, more or less, at the far end, where there was a fireplace but no fire. As I approached, Mrs. Vail said, "Well?"

"It was Dinah Utley," I said.

"What—how—"

I glanced around. "I'm not intruding?"

"It's all right," Jimmy Vail said. He was standing with his back to the fireplace. "They know about it. My wife's daughter, Margot Tedder. Her brother, Ralph Purcell. Her attorney, Andrew Frost."

"They know about Nero Wolfe," Mrs. Vail said. "My children and my brother were asking questions, and we thought we had better tell them. Then when this—Dinah—and we'll be asked where we were last night . . . I decided my lawyer ought to know about it and about Nero Wolfe. It was Dinah?"

"Yes."

"She was run over by a car?" From Andrew Frost, the lawyer. He looked a little like the man of bronze who was standing behind his chair, Abraham Lincoln, but he had no beard and his hair was gray; and on his feet probably he wasn't quite as tall. Presumably he had learned how

Dinah had died by phoning White Plains, or from a broadcast.

"She was run over by *her* car," I said.

"Her own car?"

I faced Mrs. Vail, who was sitting on a couch, slumped against cushions. "On behalf of Mr. Wolfe," I told her, "I owe you two pieces of information. One, I looked at the corpse and identified it as Dinah Utley. Two, I told the District Attorney that I saw her yesterday afternoon when she came to Mr. Wolfe's office in connection with a matter you had consulted him about. That's all. I refused to tell him what the matter was or anything about it. That's all I owe you, but if you want to know how and when and where Dinah died I'll throw that in. Do you want it?"

"Yes. First when."

"Between nine o'clock last evening and three o'clock this morning. That may be narrowed down later. It was murder, because her own car ran across her chest and was there, nosed into a roadside opening, when the body was found. There was a bruise on the side of her head; she was probably hit with something and knocked out before the car was run over her. Then the—"

I stopped because she had made a sound, call it a moan, and shut her eyes. "Do you have to be utterly brutal?" Margot Tedder asked. The daughter, a couple of years younger than her brother Noel, was at the other end of the couch. From hearsay, she was a pain in the neck who kept her chin up so she could look down her nose; from my personal knowledge, she was a nice slender specimen with real possibilities if she would round out a little and watch the corners of her mouth, and, seeing her walk or dance, you might have thought her hips were in a cast.

"I didn't do it," I told her. "I'm just telling it."

"You haven't said where," Jimmy Vail said. "Where was it?"

Mrs. Vail's eyes had opened, and I preferred to tell her, since she was the client. "Iron Mine Road. That's a narrow rocky lane off of Route One Twenty-three. Route One Twenty-three goes into Route Thirty-five seven miles east of Katonah, not far from the state line."

Her eyes had widened. "My God," she said, staring at

me. *"They* killed her." She turned to Andrew Frost. "The kidnapers. They killed her." Back to me. "Then you were right, what Mr. Wolfe said about suspecting her. That's where—"

"Wait a minute, Althea," Frost commanded her. "I must speak with you privately. This is dangerous business, extremely dangerous. You should have told me Monday when you got that note. As your counselor, I instruct you to say nothing more to anyone until you have talked with me. And I don't— Where are you going?"

She had left the couch and was heading for the door. She said over her shoulder, "I'll be back," and kept going, on out. Jimmy moved. He went halfway to the door, stopped and stood, his back to us, and then came back to the fireplace. Ralph Purcell, Mrs. Vail's brother, said something to Frost and got no response. I had never seen Purcell and knew next to nothing of him, either hearsay or personal knowledge. Around fifty, take a couple of years either way, with not much hair left and a face as round as his sister's, he had a habit I had noticed: when someone started to say something he looked at someone else. If he was after an effect he got it; it made you want to say something to him and see if you could keep his eye.

Noel Tedder, who was leaning against George Washington, asked me, "What's this about suspecting her? Suspecting her of what?" The lawyer shook his head at him, and Margot said, "What's the difference now? She's dead." Purcell was looking at me, and I was deciding what to say to him and try to hold his eye when Mrs. Vail came in. She had an envelope in her hand. She came back to the couch, sat on the edge, and took papers from the envelope. Frost demanded, "What have you got there? Althea, I absolutely insist—"

"I don't care what you insist," she told him. "You're a good lawyer, Andy, Harold thought so and so do I, and I trust your advice on things you know about, you know I do, but this is different. I told you about it because you could tell me about the legal part of it, but now I don't need just *legal* advice, now that I know Dinah was killed there on Iron Mine Road. I think I need something more than legal advice, I think I need Nero Wolfe." She turned to me. "Would he come here? He wouldn't, would he?"

I shook my head. "He never leaves the house on business. If you want to see him he'll be available at six—"

"No. I don't feel like—no. I can tell you. Can't I?"

"Certainly." I got my notebook and pen from a pocket, went to a chair near the end of the couch, and sat.

She looked around. "I want you to hear it, all of you. You all knew Dinah. I'm sure you all thought of her as highly as I did—I don't mean you all liked her, that's not it, but you thought she was very competent and completely reliable. But apparently she—but wait till you hear it." She fingered in the papers, extracted one, handed it to me, and looked around again. "I've told you about the note I got Monday morning saying they had Jimmy and I would get a phone call from Mr. Knapp. Nero Wolfe has it. And I've told you, haven't I—yes, I did—that when the phone call came Monday afternoon Dinah listened in and took it down. Later she typed it from her notes, and that's it. Read it aloud, Mr. Goodwin."

A glance had shown me that the typing was the same as the note, the same faint letters, but on a better grade of paper and a different size, 8½ by 11. I read it to them:

MRS. VAIL: This is Althea Vail. Are you—
KNAPP: I'm Mr. Knapp. Did you get the note?
MRS. VAIL: Yes. This morning. Yes.
KNAPP: Is anyone else on the wire?
MRS. VAIL: No. Of course not. The note said—
KNAPP: Keep it strictly to yourself. You had better if you want to see your Jimmy again. Have you got the money?
MRS. VAIL: No, how could I? I only got the note—
KNAPP: Get it. You've got until tomorrow. Get it and put it in a suitcase. Five hundred thousand dollars in used bills, nothing bigger than a hundred. You understand that?
MRS. VAIL: Yes, I understand. But where is my husband? Is he—
KNAPP: He's perfectly all right. Safe and sound, not a scratch on him. That's absolutely straight, Mrs. Vail.

If you play it straight, you can count on us. Now listen. I don't want to talk long. Get the money and put it in a suitcase. Tomorrow evening, Tuesday, put the suitcase in the trunk of your blue sedan, and don't forget to make sure the trunk's locked. Take the Merritt Parkway. Leave it at the Westport exit, Route 33. You know Route 33?

MRS. VAIL: Yes.

KNAPP: Do you know where Fowler's Inn is?

MRS. VAIL: Yes.

KNAPP: Go to Fowler's Inn. Get there at ten o'clock tomorrow evening. Don't get there much before ten, and not any later than five after ten. Take a table on the left side and order a drink. You'll get a message. Understand?

MRS. VAIL: Yes. What kind of a message? How will I know—

KNAPP: You'll know. You're sure you understand?

MRS. VAIL: Yes. Fowler's Inn at ten o'clock tomorrow evening. But when—

KNAPP: Just do as you're told. That's all.

I looked up. "That's all."

"But my God, Mom," Noel Tedder blurted, "if you had told me!"

"Or me," Andrew Frost said grimly.

"Well?" Mrs. Vail demanded. "What could you have done? Jimmy's here, isn't he? He's here alive and well. I went to Nero Wolfe, I've told you about that, and what he did may have helped, I don't know and I don't care now."

"I think you were extremely wise," Margot Tedder said, "not to tell either of them. Mr. Frost would have tried to make you wait until he looked it up in the books. Noel would have gone to Fowler's Inn in disguise, probably with a false beard. You went, Mother? To Fowler's Inn?"

Mrs. Vail nodded. "I did exactly what he told me to. Of course Mr. Graham at the bank was suspicious—no, not suspicious, curious—and he wanted me to tell him what the money was for, but I didn't. It was my money. I got to Fowler's Inn too early, and sat in the car until ten o'clock, and then went in. I tried not to show how nervous I was, but I suppose I did; I kept looking at my watch, and at twenty after ten I was called to the phone. It was in a booth. The voice sounded like the other one, Mr. Knapp, but he didn't say. He told me to look in the Manhattan phone book where Z begins, and hung up. I looked in the phone book, and there was a note. I have it." She extracted another sheet of paper and handed it to me. "Read it, Mr. Goodwin."

"Wait a minute." It was Jimmy Vail. He had moved and was standing looking down at his wife. "I think you'd better call a halt, Al. You and I had better have a talk. Telling Goodwin all this, telling Frost—it's not Friday yet."

She lifted a hand to touch his arm. "I have to, Jimmy. I *have* to, now that Dinah—my God, they killed her! Read it, Mr. Goodwin."

It was the same typing, and on the same cheap paper as the note that had come in the mail. I read it aloud.

> Leave immediately. Speak to no one. Go to car. Read the rest of this after you are in the car. Drive to Route 7 and turn right. Beyond Weston leave Route 7 on any byroad and turn off of it in a mile or so onto some other byroad. Do this, taking turns at random, for half an hour, then return to Route 7 and go towards Danbury. A mile beyond Branchville stop at The Fatted Calf, take a table and order a drink. You'll get a message.

"I'll take that," Jimmy Vail said. "And the other one." His hand was there for them. From his tone, it seemed likely that if I tried to argue that I wanted to show them to Wolfe I would lose the debate, so I got the texts in my notebook in shorthand. That wasn't really necessary, since after years of practice I can report long conversations verbatim, but with such documents as those it was desirable. Transferring typed text to shorthand was practically automatic, so my ears could take in what Mrs. Vail was saying:

"I did what the note said. I think a car was following me all the time, but I wasn't sure. I think I didn't want to know, I didn't want to be sure. The same thing happened at The Fatted Calf, the same as Fowler's Inn. At ten minutes after eleven I was called to the phone, and the same voice told me to look in the phone book where U begins,

and there was another note." She handed it to me. "Read
it."

Same typing, same paper. I read:

> Leave immediately. Speak to no one. Read the rest of
> this in the car. Continue on Route 7 to the intersection
> with Route 35. Turn left on Route 35, and continue on
> 35 through Ridgefield. Two miles beyond Ridgefield turn
> left onto Route 123. Go 1.7 miles on Route 123 and
> turn right onto Iron Mine Road. Go slow. When a car
> behind blinks its lights three times, stop. The car will stop
> behind you. Get out and open the trunk. A man will
> approach and say, "It's time for a Knapp," and you will
> give him the suitcase. He will tell you what to do.

"He did," Mrs. Vail said. "He told me to drive straight
back to New York, here, without stopping. He told me
not to tell anyone anything until Jimmy came back or he
would never come back. He said he would be back within
twenty-four hours. And he was! He is! Thank God!" She
put out a hand to touch her Jimmy, but had to stretch
because he was sticking with me to get the notes. I was
getting the last one in my notebook. The Tedder son and
daughter were saying something, and so was Andrew
Frost. Finishing with my shorthand, I reached around
Jimmy to hand the papers to Mrs. Vail. He had a hand
there, but I ignored it, and she took them. She spoke to
me.

"You see why I had to tell Nero Wolfe. Or you."

"I can guess," I told her. "Mr. Wolfe told you we suspected that Dinah Utley was implicated in the kidnaping.
Now I tell you that her body was found on Iron Mine
Road, at the spot where you turned over the suitcase, or
near there. That complicates your problem when Westchester County comes to ask you about Dinah Utley and
why you had her go to see Mr. Wolfe, especially if you
and your husband still want to save it until Friday.
Haven't they been here yet?"

"No."

"They soon will be. As for Mr. Wolfe and me, we'll
stand pat until eleven o'clock Friday morning. He made it
eleven o'clock because that's when he comes down from
the plant rooms. As for you and your husband, and now

also your son and daughter and brother and lawyer, you'll have to decide for yourselves. It's risky to withhold information material to a murder, but if it's for self-protection from a real danger, if you think Mr. Knapp meant business when he told your husband he'd regret it if he or you spilled it before Friday, I doubt if you'll have any serious trouble. Is that what you want from Mr. Wolfe or me?"

"No." She had the papers back in the envelope and was clutching it. "Only partly that. I want to know why you thought Dinah was implicated."

"Naturally." I put the notebook back in my pocket. "You didn't see her there? At Iron Mine Road?"

"No, of course not."

"Not of course not, since she *was* there. Was the man alone in the car behind you?"

"I didn't see anyone else. It was dark. I wasn't—I wasn't caring if there was anyone else."

"What did the man look like?"

"I don't know. He had a coat and a hat pulled down, and his face was covered with something, all but his eyes."

"Who left first, him or you?"

"I did. He told me to. I had to go on up the road to find a place to turn around."

"Was his car still there when you came back past the spot?"

"Yes. He had it up against the bank so I could get by."

"Did you see any other car anywhere on that road?"

"No." She gestured impatiently. "What has this to do with Dinah?"

"Nothing," Noel Tedder said. "He's a detective. It's his nature. He's putting you through the wringer."

"I insist," Andrew Frost said emphatically, "that this is ill-advised. *Very* ill-advised. You're making a mistake, Althea. Don't you agree, Jimmy?"

Jimmy was back at the fireplace. "Yes," he said. "I agree."

"But Jimmy, you must see," she protested. "She was *there!* And they killed her! You must see I want to know why Nero Wolfe suspected her!" To me: "Why did he?"

I shook my head. "I only run errands. But you're wel-

come to a hint." I stood up. "That phone talk you had
with Mr. Knapp Monday afternoon, that Dinah listened
to and took down. May I see the machine she typed it
on?"

The three men spoke at once. Jimmy Vail and Andrew
Frost both said, "No!" and Noel Tedder said, "Didn't I
tell you?" Mrs. Vail ignored them and asked, "Why?"

"I'll probably tell you after I see it. And I may have a
suggestion to make. Is it here?"

"It's in my study." She arose. "Will you tell me why
you suspected Dinah?"

"I'll either tell you or you'll have a healthy idea."

"All right, come with me." She moved, paying no attention to protests from the men. I followed her out and
along the hall to a door frame where she pressed a button. The door of a do-it-yourself elevator slid open, and
we entered. That elevator was a much newer and neater
job than the one in Wolfe's house that took him up to his
room or the roof. No noise or jiggle. When it stopped and
the door opened, she stepped out and led the way down
the hall, some narrower than the one below. The room
we entered was much smaller than the Harold F. Tedder
library. Inside, I stopped for a glance around—that's
habit. Two desks, one large and one small, shelves with
books and magazines, filing cabinet, a large wall mirror, a
television set on a table, framed photographs. Mrs. Vail
had crossed to the small desk. She turned and said, "It's
not here! The typewriter."

I went to her. At the end of the desk was a typewriter
stand on casters. There was nothing on it. She had turned
again and was staring at it. There were only two questions worth asking, and I asked them.

"Is it always kept here, or is it sometimes taken to another room?"

"Never. It is kept here."

"When did you last see it here?"

"I don't—I'd have to think. I haven't been in here
today, until just now, when I came to get this envelope. I
didn't notice it was gone. Sometime yesterday—I'd have
to think. I can't imagine . . ."

"Someone may have borrowed it." I went to the door
and turned. "I'll report to Mr. Wolfe. If he has anything

to say we'll ring you. The main thing is we'll stay put until Friday unless you—"

"But you're going to tell me why you suspected Dinah!"

"Not now. Find the typewriter, and we'll see." I left. As I went down the hall her voice followed me, but I kept going. I was in no mood for talk. I should never have mentioned the typewriter, since it had nothing to do with the job Wolfe had been paid for, but I had wanted to get a sample from it to take along. Noel Tedder had been right; I was a detective, and it was my nature. Nuts. Skipping the elevator, I took the stairs, three flights down, and when I reached the ground floor the square-faced female appeared through an arch. She got my coat and held it, and went and opened the door; and there entering the vestibule was Ben Dykes, head of the Westchester County detectives.

I said, "Hello there. Get stopped for speeding?"

He said, "I've been in the park feeding pigeons. I didn't want to butt in."

"That's the spirit. I fully appreciate it. May your tribe increase." I circled around him, on out, and headed for 81st Street, where I had left the car.

5

At six o'clock, when the sound came of Wolfe's elevator descending, I was in my chair in the office, my feet up on the desk, my weight on the base of my spine, and my head back.

For twenty minutes I had been playing a guessing game, which was all it amounted to, since we had nothing to do but sit on it, and since I didn't have enough bones to make a skeleton, let alone meat. But some day all the details of the Jimmy Vail kidnaping, including the murder of Dinah Utley, would be uncovered, whether they got Mr. Knapp or not, and if I could dope it here and now with what little I had, and it turned out that I was right, I could pin a medal on myself. So I worked at it.

Question: Was Dinah Utley in on it?

Answer: Certainly. She typed the note that came by mail and those Mrs. Vail found in the phone books.

Q: Who took the typewriter?

A: Dinah Utley. When she learned that Mrs. Vail had gone to Nero Wolfe, and when I took her prints and asked about her fingers, she got leery and ditched the typewriter.

Q: Was she with the man who got the suitcase from Mrs. Vail?

A: No. She was in her car somewhere along Iron Mine Road, and when Mrs. Vail drove back out she drove on in. She wanted to be sure of getting her cut. The man who had got the suitcase, probably Mr. Knapp, didn't care for that and killed her.

Q: Was anyone at the Vail house in on it besides Dinah Utley?

A: Yes. Jimmy Vail. He kidnaped himself. He had another man in it too, because he wasn't Mr. Knapp on the phone; it would have been too risky trying to disguise his voice. But he might have been the man who got the suitcase and therefore the man who killed Dinah Utley. That disagrees with the "probably Mr. Knapp" in the preceding answer, but we're not in court. Items: Jimmy scooted from this office when he heard Wolfe tell Mrs. Vail that we suspected Dinah Utley, he told her she'd better call a halt when she produced the notes she had got from the phone books, and he tried to take the notes from me. Also his reactions in general. Also his insisting on saving it until Friday.

Q: Why did he have Dinah in on it?

A: Pass. No bone. A dozen possible reasons.

Q: Wouldn't he have been a sap to have Dinah type the notes on that typewriter?

A: No. The state of mind Mrs. Vail would be in when she got the note by mail, he knew she wouldn't inspect the typing. When he got back he would destroy the notes. He would say he had promised Mr. Knapp he would and he was afraid not to. She had to use *some* typewriter, and buying or renting or borrowing one might have been riskier. Using that one and destroying the notes, there would be no risk at all. He wanted to take the notes from me.

Q: Could Ralph Purcell or Andrew Frost or Noel Tedder be Mr. Knapp?

A: No. Mrs. Vail knows their voices too well.

Q: Friday, if not sooner, Jimmy will have to open up. Where and how they took him, and kept him, and turned him loose. With the cops and the FBI both at him, won't he be sure to slip?

A: No. He'll say they blindfolded him and he doesn't know where they took him and kept him. Last night, early this morning, they took him somewhere blindfolded and turned him loose.

Q: Then how are they going to uncover it so you can check it with these guesses and get your medal? How would you?

I was working on that one when the sound of the elevator came. Wolfe entered, crossed to his desk, sat, and said, "Report?"

I took my feet down and pulled my spine up. "Yes, sir. It's Dinah Utley. I told District Attorney Clark Hobart that I had seen her yesterday afternoon when she came here in connection with a job Mrs. Vail had hired you to do. When he asked me what the job was it would have been rude just to tell him to go to hell, so I said that if he would tell me when and where and how Dinah Utley had died, and if I relayed it to you, you would decide what to do. Of course there's no point in relaying it, since you said we don't care what happened to her and are not concerned. I have informed Mrs. Vail and told her we'll stand pat until eleven a.m. Friday."

I swiveled, pulled the typewriter around, inserted paper and carbons, got the notebook from my pocket, and hit the keys. Perfect harmony. It helps a lot, with two people as much together as he and I were, if they understand each other. He understood that I was too strong-minded to add another word unless he told me to, and I understood that he was too pigheaded to tell me to. Of course I had to keep busy; I couldn't just sit and be strong-minded. I typed the texts of the two notes and other jottings I had made in my book, then went and opened the safe and got the note Mr. Knapp had sent by mail. It seemed likely that Jimmy Vail would be wanting it, and it was quite possible that developments would make it desirable for us to have something to show someone. I clipped the note to the edge of my desk pad, propped the pad against the back of a chair, got one of the cameras —the Tollens, which I have better luck with—and took half a dozen shots. All this time, of course, Wolfe was at his book, with no glance at me. I had returned the note to the safe and put the camera away, and was putting the film in a drawer, when the doorbell rang. I went to the hall door for a look, turned, and told Wolfe, "Excuse me for interrupting. Ben Dykes, head of the Westchester County detectives. He was there this afternoon. He's a little fatter than when you saw him some years ago at the home of James U. Sperling near Chappaqua."

He finished a sentence before he turned his head. "Confound it," he muttered. "Must I?"

"No. I can tell him we're not concerned. Of course in a week or so they might get desperate and take us to White Plains on a warrant."

"You haven't reported."

"I reported all you said you wanted."

"That's subdolous. Let him in."

As I went to the front I was making a mental note not to look up "subdolous." That trick of his, closing an argument by using a word he knew damn well I had never heard, was probably subdolous. I opened the door, told Dykes he had been expected as I took his coat and hat, which was true, and ushered him to the office. Three steps in, he stopped for a glance around. "Very nice," he said. "Nice work if you can get it. You don't remember me, Mr. Wolfe." Wolfe said he did remember him and told him to be seated, and Dykes went to the red leather chair.

"I didn't think it was necessary to get a local man to come along," he said, "since all I'm after is a little information. Goodwin has told you about Dinah Utley. When he was up there he was the last one who had seen her alive as far as we knew, him and you when she was here yesterday afternoon, but since then I've spoken with two people who had seen her after that. But you know how it is with a murder, you have to start somewhere, and that's what I'm doing, trying to get a start, and maybe you can help. Goodwin said Dinah Utley came here yesterday because Mrs. Vail told her to. Is that right?"

"Yes."

"Well, of course I'm not asking what Mrs. Vail wanted you to do for her, I understand that was confidential, and I'm only asking about Dinah Utley. I'm not even asking what you said to her, I'm only asking what she said to you. That may be important, since she was murdered just eight or nine hours after that. What did she say?"

A corner of Wolfe's mouth was up a little. "Admirable," he declared. "Competent and admirable."

Dykes got his notebook out. "She said that?"

"No. I say it. Your demand couldn't be better organized or better put. Admirable. You have the right to expect a comparable brevity and lucidity from me." He turned a hand over. "Mr. Dykes. I can't tell you what Miss Utley said to me yesterday without divulging what Mrs. Vail has told me in confidence. Of course that wasn't a privileged communication; I'm not a member of the bar, I'm a detective; and if what Mrs. Vail told me is material to your investigation of a murder I withhold it at my peril. The question, is it material, can be answered now only by me; you can't answer it because you don't know what she told me. To my present knowledge, the answer is no."

"You're withholding it?"

"Yes."

"You refuse to tell me what Dinah Utley said to you yesterday?"

"Yes."

"Or anything about what she came here for?"

"Yes."

Dykes stood up. "As you say, at your peril." He glanced around. "Nice place you've got here. Nice to see you again." He turned and headed for the door. I followed him out and down the hall. As I held his coat for him he said, "At your peril too, Goodwin, huh?" I thanked him for warning me as I gave him his hat, and asked him to give Captain Saunders my love.

When I returned to the office Wolfe had his book open again. Always he is part mule, but sometimes he is all mule. He still didn't know when or where or how Dinah Utley had died, and he knew I did know, and he had no idea how much or little risk he was running to earn the rest of that sixty grand, but by gum he wasn't going to budge. He wasn't going to admit that we cared what had happened to her because he had been childish enough to tell me we didn't.

At the dinner table, in between bites of deviled grilled lamb kidneys with a sauce he and Fritz had invented, he explained why it was that all you needed to know about any human society was what they ate. If you knew what they ate you could deduce everything else—culture, philosophy, morals, politics, everything. I enjoyed it because the kidneys were tender and tasty and that sauce is one of Fritz' best, but I wondered how you would make out if you tried to deduce everything about Wolfe by knowing what he had eaten in the past ten years. I decided you would deduce that he was dead.

After dinner I went out. Wednesday was poker night, and that Wednesday Saul Panzer was the host, at his one-man apartment on the top floor of a remodeled house on 38th Street between Lexington and Third. You'll meet Saul further on. If you've already met him you know why I would have liked to have an hour alone with him, to give him the picture and see if he agreed with me about Jimmy Vail. It was just as well I couldn't have the hour, because if Saul had agreed with me I would have had a personal problem; it would no longer have been just my private guess. Jimmy Vail was responsible for our holding it back until Friday, and if he had killed Dinah Utley he was making monkeys of us. Of course that would serve Wolfe right, but how about me? It affected my poker, with Saul right there, but four other men were there also so I couldn't tell him. Saul, who misses nothing, saw that I was off my game and made remarks about it. It didn't affect his game any. He usually wins, and that night he raked it in. When we quit at the usual deadline, two o'clock, he had more than a hundred bucks of my money, and I was in no mood to stay and confide in him as an old and trusted friend.

Thursday, the morning after a late session of hard, tight poker, I don't turn out until nine or nine-thirty unless something important is cooking, but that Thursday I found myself lying on my back with my eyes wide open before eight. It was getting on my nerves. I said aloud, "Goddam Jimmy Vail anyhow," swung my legs around, and got erect.

I like to walk. I liked to walk in woods and pastures when I was a kid in Ohio, and now I like to walk even more on Manhattan sidewalks. If you don't walk much you wouldn't know, but the angle you get on people and things when you're walking is absolutely different from the one you get when you're in a car or in anything else that does the moving for you. So after washing and shaving and dressing and eating breakfast and reading about Dinah Utley in the *Times,* nothing I didn't already know, I buzzed the plant rooms on the house phone to tell Wolfe I was going out on a personal errand and would be back by noon, and went.

Of course you don't learn anything about people in general by walking around taking them in; you only learn things about this one or that one. I learned something that morning about a girl in a gray checked suit who caught her heel in a grating on Second Avenue in the Eighties. No girl I had ever known would have done what she did. Maybe no other girl in the world would. But I shouldn't have got started about walking. I mentioned walking only to explain how it happened that at a quarter past eleven I entered a drugstore at the corner of 54th Street and Eighth Avenue, sat at the counter, and requested a glass of milk. As it was brought and I took a sip, a Broadway type came in and got on the stool next to me and said to the soda jerk, "Cuppa coffee, Sam. You heard about Jimmy Vail?"

"Where would I hear about Jimmy Vail?" Sam demanded, getting a cup. "All I hear is step on it. What about Jimmy Vail?"

"He died. It was on the radio just now. Found him dead on the floor with a statue on top of him. You know I used to know Jimmy before he married a billion. Knew him well."

"I didn't know." Sam brought the coffee. "Too bad." A customer came to a stool down the line, and Sam moved.

I finished the glass of milk before I went to the phone

booth. I may have gulped it some, but by God I finished it. I wasn't arranging my mind; there was nothing in it to arrange; I was just drinking milk. When I went to the phone booth I got out a dime and started my hand to the slot but pulled it back. Not good enough. A voice on a phone is all right up to a point, but I might decide to go beyond that point, and a little more walking might help. I returned the dime to my pocket, departed, walked seven blocks crosstown and ten blocks downtown, entered the marble lobby of a building, and took an elevator.

I gave the receptionist on the twentieth floor a nod and went on by. Lon Cohen's room, with his name on the door but no title, was two doors this side of the *Gazette*'s publisher's. I don't remember a time that I have ever entered it and he wasn't on the phone, and that time was no exception. He darted a glance at me and went on talking, and I took the chair at the end of his desk and noted that he showed no sign of being short on sleep, though he had left Saul's place the same time I had, a little after two. His little dark face was neat and smooth, and his dark brown, deep-set eyes were clear and keen. When he had finished on the phone he turned to me and shook his head.

"Sorry, I've banked it. I guess I could spare a ducat."

He had been the only winner last night besides Saul. "I wouldn't want to strap you," I said. "A dime would see me through the week. But first, what about Jimmy Vail?"

"Oh." He cocked his head. "Is Wolfe looking for a job, or has he got one?"

"Neither one. I'm interested personally. I was taking a walk and heard something. I could wait and buy a paper, but I'm curious. What about him?"

"He's dead."

"So I heard. How?"

"He was found—you know about the Harold F. Tedder library."

"Yeah. Statues."

"He was found there a little after nine o'clock this morning by his stepdaughter, Margot Tedder. On the floor, with Benjamin Franklin on him. Benjamin Franklin in bronze, a copy of the one in Philadelphia by John

Thomas Macklin. That would be a beautiful picture, but I don't know if we got one. I can phone downstairs."

"No, thanks. How did Benjamin Franklin get on him?"

"If we only knew that and knew it first. You got any ideas?"

"No. What do you know?"

"Damn little. Nothing. I can phone downstairs and see if anything more is in, but I doubt it. We've got five men on it, but you know how the cops are, and the DA, when it's people in that bracket. They don't even snarl, they just button their lips."

"You must know *some*thing. Like how long he'd been dead."

"We don't. We will in time for the three-o'clock." The phone buzzed. He got it, said "Yes" twice and "No" four times, and returned to me. "Your turn, Archie. Your fee's showing, or Wolfe's fee is. Yesterday morning the body of Mrs. Vail's secretary is found in a ditch in Westchester. This morning the body of her husband is found in her library, and here you come—not on the phone, in person. So of course Wolfe has been hired by someone. When? Yesterday? About the secretary?"

I eyed him. "I could give you a whole front page."

"I'll settle for half. Don't pin me to the wall with your steely eyes. I'm sensitive. You know who killed the secretary."

"No. I thought I did, but not now. What I've got may break any minute—or it may not. If I give it to you now you'll have to save it until I give the word—unless it breaks, of course. This is personal. Mr. Wolfe doesn't even know I'm here."

"Okay. I'll save it."

"You don't mean maybe."

"No. I'll save it unless it breaks."

"Then get pencil and paper. Jimmy Vail was expected home from the country Sunday night but didn't come. Monday morning Mrs. Vail got a note in the mail saying she could have him back for five hundred grand and she would get a phone call from Mr. Knapp. I have a photograph of the note, taken by me, and I may let you have a print if you'll help me mark a deck of cards so I can win

my money back from Saul. How would you like to run a
good picture of that note, exclusive?"

"I'd help you mark ten decks of cards. A hundred. Is
this straight, Archie?"

"Yes."

"My God. That 'Knapp' is beautiful. How did he spell
it?"

I spelled it. "He phoned Monday afternoon and told
her to get the money, put it in a suitcase, put the suitcase
in the trunk of her blue sedan, and Tuesday evening drive
to Fowler's Inn on Route Thirty-three, arriving at ten
o'clock. She did so. At Fowler's Inn she was called to the
phone and was told, probably the same voice, to look in
the phone book where Z begins. There was a note there
giving instructions. I haven't—"

"Beautiful," Lon said. His pencil was moving fast.

"Not bad. Don't interrupt, I'm in a hurry. I haven't got
a picture of that note, but I have the text, taken from the
original by me. The notes were typewritten. Following the
instructions, she drove around a while and got to The
Fatted Calf around eleven o'clock. There she got another
phone call and was told to look in the phone book where
U begins. Another note, same typewriting—I have the
text. More instructions. Following them, she took Route
Seven to Route Thirty-five, Route Thirty-five to Route
One Twenty-three, and Route One Twenty-three to Iron
Mine Road, which is all rock and a yard wide. She turned
into it. When a car—"

"Dinah Utley," Lon said. "The secretary. Her body
was found on Iron Mine Road."

"Don't interrupt. When a car behind her blinked its
lights she stopped and got out and got the suitcase from
the trunk. A man with only his eyes uncovered came
from the other car, took the suitcase, and told her to go
straight home, stop nowhere, and say nothing, which she
did. Around seven-thirty yesterday morning her husband
phoned her from their place in the country and said the
kidnapers had let him go in one piece and he would come
to town as soon as he cleaned up and ate. He also said
they had told him to keep the lid on for forty-eight hours
or he would regret it, and he was going to and expected
her to. I don't know exactly when he arrived at the house

on Fifth Avenue, but it must have been around ten o'clock."

I stood up. "Okay, that's it. I've got to go. If your sheet prints even a hint of it before I give the word, I'll write a letter to the editor and feed your eyes to the cat. If and when I give the word, there is to be no mention of Nero Wolfe or me. If it breaks, about the kidnaping, before I give the word, you'll still be out in front with a lot of facts the others won't have. I'll be seeing you."

"Wait a minute!" Lon was up. "You know how hot this is. It could burn my ass to cinders."

"It sure could. Then you couldn't help me mark a deck."

"How solid is it?"

"It isn't. There's an alternative. Either it's good as gold, every word, or Mrs. Jimmy Vail is unquestionably a double-breasted liar and almost certainly a murderer. If the latter, she'll be in no position to burn even your ears, let alone your ass. If she killed Dinah Utley, who killed Jimmy? Benjamin Franklin?" I turned to go.

"Damn it, listen!" He had my arm. "Was Dinah Utley with Mrs. Vail Tuesday night in the blue sedan?"

"No. For either alternative, that's positive. Dinah's own car was there at Iron Mine Road. That's the crop for now, Lon. I just wanted to burn a bridge. You could ask questions for an hour, but I haven't got an hour."

I went. Out to the elevator, down to the lobby, out to the sidewalk; and I started walking again. A taxi wouldn't have been much quicker, and I preferred to be on my feet. Down Lexington Avenue to 35th Street, and crosstown to the old brownstone. I mounted the stoop, let myself in with my key, put my coat on a hanger, and went to the office. Wolfe was at his desk, pouring beer.

"Good afternoon," I said. "Did you turn on the radio for the twelve o'clock news?"

"Yes."

"Did it mention Jimmy Vail?"

"Yes."

I went to my desk and sat. "I dropped in so you could have the satisfaction of firing me face to face. I have disobeyed orders. I am disloyal. I have betrayed your trust. I just told Lon Cohen about the kidnaping of Jimmy

Vail. Not for publication; he won't use it until I say he can. I didn't mention Mrs. Vail's hiring you. I kept you out of it. I'm not quitting, you're firing me, so I'm entitled to two months' severance pay."

He lifted the glass and drank. The idea is to drink when there is still an inch of foam so it will get on his lips and he can lick it off. He licked it off and put the glass down. "Is this flummery?" he demanded.

"No, sir. It's straight. If you want me to tell you why I did it, I will, but not as an excuse, just as information. Do you want it?"

"Yes."

"It was getting too hot. I knew too much that you didn't know. You wouldn't take what I had got at White Plains, and you knew darned well I had seen Mrs. Vail on my way back, and you wouldn't take what I had got there either. From what——"

"I did not refuse to listen to you."

"Nuts. You know as well as I do how it stood. You had said we didn't care what had happened to Dinah Utley and we were not concerned. Will it help to chew at that?"

"No."

"Okay. What I had got had made me decide that Jimmy had probably kidnaped himself, and he had killed Dinah Utley, and he was making monkeys of us. So I was stuck. I had to give in and say, please Mr. Wolfe, put your book down for a while and kindly permit me to tell you what happened yesterday so you can decide what to do. When you came down at eleven o'clock. You know how I liked that. I wasn't going to sit here on my rump all morning looking forward to it, so I went for a walk, and at eighteen minutes past eleven I heard a man tell another man that Jimmy Vail had been found dead on the floor of the library, where I had been yesterday afternoon."

I paused for dramatic effect. "So where was I? If Homicide hadn't already learned that I had been there yesterday in conference with the whole damn family, they soon would. Cramer himself might already be here ringing the bell. When he asked me what I was doing there, if I told him, I would be ditching our commitment to Mrs.

Vail, and if I didn't tell him, I would be in for a picnic and the least I could expect would be losing my license. It wouldn't help any to come and say, please, Mr. Wolfe, even if you're not concerned kindly permit me to tell you what has happened because I'm in a jam. What could you do? I had to handle it myself, and I did. I went and did something you had told me not to do. I told Lon Cohen about the kidnaping. Then I came and saw that Cramer or Stebbins wasn't here, since there was no police car out front, and entered. Now you fire me and I go. Fast. One will get you a thousand that no one will find me before eleven o'clock tomorrow morning, the deadline." I arose.

"Sit down," he growled.

"No. Cramer or Stebbins may be here any minute."

"He won't be admitted."

"They'll cover the house front and back and come back with a warrant." I moved.

"Stop!" he bellowed. "Very well," he said. "You leave me no choice. I concede that we care what happened to Miss Utley and we are concerned. Report in full."

"If I'm fired why should I report?"

"You are not fired. Confound you, report!"

"It's too late. I'd be interrupted. The doorbell might ring any second."

He glared at me, then turned his head to glare at the clock. He made fists of his hands and glared at them, then used them to push his chair back. He got up and headed for the door, and when he reached the hall he roared, "Fritz!" The door to the kitchen swung open, and Fritz appeared. Wolfe was moving to the front, to the rack. He got his coat off the hanger and turned.

"Are the mussels open?"

"No, sir. It's only—"

"Don't open them. Keep them. Archie and I are going out. We'll be back for lunch tomorrow. Keep the door bolted."

Fritz gawked. "But—but—" He was speechless.

"If anyone inquires, you can't tell tell him where we are, since you won't know." He found the armholes of the coat I had taken and was holding. "Lunch at the usual time tomorrow."

"But you must have a bag—"

"I'll manage. Tell Theodore. You know what a search warrant is. If a policeman comes with one admit him, and stay with him. Archie?"

I had my coat on and the door open. He crossed the sill, and as I followed I shut the door. As we descended the stoop I asked, "The car?" and he said no, and at the bottom he turned right, toward Ninth Avenue. But we didn't reach Ninth Avenue. Halfway there he turned right and started up a stoop of a brownstone the same size and color and age as his, but it had a vestibule. He had used his vestibule to enlarge the hall years ago. He pushed the button, and in a moment the door was opened by a dark-haired woman with fine frontage to whom we had sent orchids now and then for the past ten years. She was a little startled at sight of us.

"Why, Mr. Wolfe . . . Mr. Goodwin . . . come in. You want to see the doctor?"

We entered, and she closed the door. "Not professionally," Wolfe said. "And briefly. Here will do."

"Of course. Certainly." She was flustered. I had been there off and on, but Wolfe hadn't; Doc Vollmer had come to him when required. She went down the hall and opened a door and disappeared, and in a minute Vollmer came—a sad-looking little guy with lots of forehead and not much jaw. He had once taken twenty-two stitches in my side where a character with a knife had gone wide enough but not deep enough.

He approached. "Well, well! Come in, come in!"

"We have come to impose on you, Doctor," Wolfe said. "We need a room to sit in the rest of today and beds for tonight. We need enough food to sustain us until tomorrow. Can you oblige us?"

Vollmer wasn't startled; he was merely stunned. "Why —of course—you mean for you? You and Archie?"

"Yes. We expected a troublesome visitor, and we fled. By tomorrow he will be less troublesome. We want seclusion until then. If it would inconvenience you beyond tolerance . . ."

"No, of course not." He smiled. "I'm honored. I'm flattered. I'm afraid the food won't be quite . . . I have no Fritz. Will you need a phone in the room?"

"No, just the room."

"Then, if you'll excuse me—I have a patient in my office—"

He went back to the door and in, and in a couple of minutes the dark-haired woman, whose name was Helen Gillard, came out. She asked us to come with her, trying to sound as if it was perfectly natural for a couple of neighbors to drop in and request board and lodging, and led the way to the stairs. She took us up two flights and down a hall to the rear, and into a room with two windows and a big bed and walls covered with pictures of boats and baseball players and boys and girls. Bill Vollmer, whom I had once showed how to take fingerprints, was away at school. Helen asked, "Will you come down for lunch or shall I bring trays?"

"Later," Wolfe said. "Thank you. Mr. Goodwin will tell you."

"Can I bring you anything?"

Wolfe said no, and she went. She left the door open, and I went and closed it. We removed our coats, and I found hangers in a closet. Wolfe stood and looked around. It was hopeless. There were three chairs. The seats of two of them were about half as wide as his fanny, and the third one had arms and it would be a squeeze. He went to the bed, sat on the edge, took his shoes off, twisted around, stretched out with his head on the pillow, shut his eyes, and spoke.

"Report."

6

At 12:35 P.M. Friday, Inspector Cramer of Homicide West, seated in the red leather chair, took a mangled unlit cigar from his mouth and said, "I still want to know where you and Goodwin have been and what you've done the past twenty-four hours."

The only objection to telling him was that he would have gone or sent someone to check, and Doc Vollmer was a busy man, so it would have been a poor return for his hospitality. As for the hospitality, I had no kick coming, having been given a perfectly good bed in a spare room, but Wolfe had had a few difficulties. Books to read, but no chair upstairs big enough to take him, and he won't read lying down. No pajamas big enough for him, so he had to sleep in his underwear. Grub not bad enough to take credit for facing up to hardship, but not good enough to please the palate; only one brand of beer, and not his. Pillows too soft to use only one and too thick to use two. Towels either too little or too big. Soap that smelled like tuberoses (he said), and he uses geranium. He really bore up well for his first day and night away from home in more than a year; he was glum, of course, as you would be if you were forced to skedaddle, without stopping to take a toothbrush, by circumstances you weren't to blame for.

We had not phoned Fritz to find out if there had been any callers because we didn't know much about modern electronics, and who does? We knew tracing a phone call wasn't as simple as it used to be, but they might have a tame neutron or positron or some other tron that could camp inside Wolfe's number and tell where a call came from. For news there were the papers, Thursday evening and Friday morning. Not a word in the *Gazette* about kidnaping; Lon had kept it; and nothing in the *Times* Friday morning or on the radio at eleven o'clock. There was plenty about Jimmy Vail, but the main fact was still as I had got it from Lon: Margot Tedder had entered the library at 9:05 Thursday morning and found him there on the floor underneath Benjamin Franklin. The bronze statue had flattened his chest.

Five people, not one, had last seen him alive Wednesday evening—his wife; her son and daughter, Noel and Margot Tedder; her brother, Ralph Purcell; and her attorney, Andrew Frost. They had all been in the library after dinner (subject of the family conference not mentioned), and shortly after ten o'clock Jimmy Vail, saying that he hadn't slept much for three days (reason not given), had stretched out on the couch and gone to sleep. He had still been there an hour later, sound asleep, when they broke it up and left. Noel and Margot Tedder and Ralph Purcell had gone up to bed, and Mrs. Vail and Andrew Frost had gone up to her study. Around midnight Frost had left, and Mrs. Vail had gone to bed. Evidently she too had been short on sleep, for she had still been in bed when her son and daughter came to her room Thursday morning to tell her about Jimmy.

Everyone in the house, of course including the servants, had known that Benjamin Franklin was wobbly. The *Gazette* had a piece by an expert about the different methods of fastening the bronze feet of a man to the base he stands on. He hadn't been permitted to examine the statue that had toppled onto Jimmy Vail, but he said the trouble couldn't have been a loose nut; his guess was that the bolt or bolts had had a flaw and had cracked at some time when the statue was being handled. It was quite possible, he said, that Jimmy Vail, half aroused from a deep sleep, on his way across the room to the door, had lost his balance and grabbed at the statue and pulled it down on him. I thought it was darned decent of the *Gazette* to run the piece. A good murder or suspicion of one will sell thousands of extra papers, and here they were promoting the idea that it had been accidental. They had got the picture Lon had said would be beautiful, of Benjamin Franklin on top of Jimmy Vail.

There were no quotes from any members of the family. Mrs. Vail was in bed under a doctor's care, inaccessible. Andrew Frost wasn't seeing reporters, but he had told the police that when he left the house around midnight, unescorted, he had not stopped at the library on his way out.

As I have said, there was nothing new on the radio at eleven o'clock Friday morning. At 11:10 I phoned Homicide West from Doc Vollmer's office downstairs—he was at the hospital—and told the desk man to tell Inspector Cramer that Nero Wolfe had some information for him regarding Jimmy Vail. At 11:13 I called the District Attorney's office at White Plains, got an assistant DA, and told him to tell Hobart that Wolfe had decided to answer any questions he might care to ask. At 11:18 I rang the *Gazette,* got Lon Cohen, and told him it was all his and would probably soon be everybody's, and he could even use our names as the source if he spelled them right. Of course he wanted more, but I hung up. At 11:24 we thanked Helen Gillard and asked her to thank the doctor for us, left the house, walked sixty yards to Wolfe's, found the door was bolted, pushed the button and were admitted by Fritz, and learned that Sergeant Purley Stebbins had come yesterday ten minutes after we left, and Inspector Cramer had come at six o'clock. No search warrant, but Cramer had phoned at 8:43 and again at 10:19. At the office door Wolfe asked about the mussels, and Fritz said they were in perfect condition. Wolfe was at his desk with his eyes closed, in the only chair that will really do, sitting and breathing, and I was at my desk opening the mail, when the doorbell rang and I went. It was Inspector Cramer, his rugged pink face a little pinker than normal and his burly shoulders hunched a little. When I let him in he didn't even give me an eye, but kept going, to the office, and as I followed, after closing the door, I heard him rasping.

"Where have you and Goodwin been since yesterday noon?"

Fifty minutes later, as I have said, at 12:35 P.M., he demanded, "I still want to know where you and Goodwin have been and what you've done the past twenty-four hours."

We had opened the bag. Most of the talking had been done by me because the whole world knows—well, six or eight people—that the only difference between me and a tape recorder is that you can ask me questions. And for some of it—the White Plains part and the session in the Harold F. Tedder library—Wolfe hadn't been present. We had handed over the note that had come in the mail, the original, and my transcriptions, carbons, of the other two notes and the telephone conversation between Mrs. Vail and Mr. Knapp. I did make a few improvements on Wolfe's phrasing, and mine too, by making it emphatic that the main point had been, first, to get Jimmy Vail back alive, and then to protect him and Mrs. Vail by keeping his promise to the kidnapers. Of course Cramer landed on that with both feet. Why had we gone on protecting Vail for twenty-four hours after he was dead? Obviously, so Wolfe could hang onto the money he already had in the bank. Withholding information vital to a murder investigation. Obstructing justice to earn a fee.

Wolfe snorted, and my feelings were hurt. There had still been Mrs. Vail to consider, and we hadn't known that Vail had been murdered. Did he? I had read an article by a statue expert which said that it could have been an accident. Wasn't it? Cramer didn't say, but he didn't have to; his being there was enough to show that it was open, though maybe not open-and-shut. He said we had of course seen the statement of the District Attorney's office in the morning paper that the apparent cause of Vail's death was the statue falling on him, that a final determination would be made when the autopsy had been completed, and that a thorough investigation was being made. Then he took the chewed unlit cigar from his mouth and said he still wanted to know where we had been the past twenty-four hours.

Wolfe would not be riled. He was back in his house, in his chair, the deadline was past, and the mussels would be ready in an hour. "As I told you," he said, "we knew we would be pestered and we decamped. Where is of no consequence. We did nothing and communicated with no one. At eleven this morning, when our obligation to Mrs. Vail had been fulfilled, Mr. Goodwin telephoned your office. You have no valid grievance. Even now you will not say that you're investigating a murder; you're trying to determine if one has been committed. A charge of obstructing justice couldn't possibly hold. Some of the questions you asked Mr. Goodwin indicated that you suspect him of trying to find the typewriter that was missing from Mrs. Vail's study. Nonsense. Since yesterday noon he has been trying to find nothing whatever, and neither have I. Our interest in the matter is ended. We have no further commitment to Mrs. Vail. We have no client. If she herself killed both Miss Utley and Mr. Vail, which seems unlikely but is not inconceivable, I owe her no service."

"She has paid you sixty thousand dollars."

"And by the terms of my employment I have earned it."

Cramer got up, came to my desk, and dropped the cigar in my wastebasket. That wasn't regular; usually he threw the cigar at it and missed. He went back and picked up his hat from the floor where he had dropped it and turned to Wolfe.

"I want a statement with nothing left out signed by you and Goodwin. At my office by four o'clock. The District

Attorney's office will probably want to see Goodwin. It would suit me fine if they want you too."

"Not everything everybody said by four o'clock," I objected. "That would be a six-hour job."

"I want the substance. All details. You can omit White Plains, we've got that from them." He turned and tramped out. By the time I had followed him to the front, shut the door after him, and returned to the office, Wolfe had his book open. I finished opening the mail and put it on his desk and then pulled the typewriter around and got out paper and carbons. That would be a job, and it was water under the bridge, since we had no case and no client. Four carbons: one for Westchester, one for the Manhattan DA, and two for us. As I rolled the paper in Wolfe's voice came at my back.

"Dendrobium chrysotoxum for Miss Gillard and Laelia purpurata for Doctor Vollmer. Tomorrow."

"Right. And Sitassia readia for you and Transcriptum underwoodum for me." I hit the keys.

With time out for lunch and a shave and a clean shirt, it was five minutes past four when I left the house, walked to 34th and Eighth Avenue for a *Gazette,* and flagged a taxi. I had made it barely in time for Wolfe to sign it before he went up to the plant rooms, but there had been interruptions. Sergeant Purley Stebbins had phoned to tell me to take the statement to the DA's office instead of Homicide West. Ben Dykes had phoned and kept me on the wire fifteen minutes and had finally settled for an appointment with Wolfe at eleven-thirty Saturday morning. Reporters from three newspapers had called, two on the phone and one in person, and had been stalled. What had stung them was on the front page of the *Gazette,* which I perused as the taxi took me downtown—the first public notice of the kidnaping of Jimmy Vail and delivery of the ransom money by his wife. Of course it didn't have the big kick of a kidnaping story, the suspense about the fate of the victim, since Jimmy had come back safe and sound, but it had the added attraction of his death by violence in his own home some fifteen hours after he returned. There were pictures of Fowler's Inn and The Fatted Calf and Iron Mine Road. Lon had hung onto it, but he had taken steps. The mention of Wolfe and me was vague and sort of gave the impression that we knew about it because we knew everything, which wouldn't hurt a bit. It was the fattest scoop I had ever given Lon, and that wouldn't hurt either. When I got to 155 Leonard Street and was taken to the room of assistant DA Mandel, he greeted me by tapping the *Gazette* that was there on his desk and demanding, "When did you give them this?" I told him ten minutes after eleven this morning.

It didn't amount to much that time. I have had several conversations in that building that lasted more than six hours, one that lasted fourteen hours, and two that ended by my being locked up as a material witness. That day Mandel and two Homicide Bureau dicks let me go in less than two hours, partly because I had the signed statement with me, partly because they weren't officially interested in the kidnaping since that had been a Westchester job, and partly because they were by no means sure Jimmy Vail's death had been a homicide and if it wasn't that would be okay with them. A dick has enough grief dealing with riffraff, and he would prefer to have no part of Tedders and Vails. So after going through the routine motions for an hour and a half they shooed me out, and at a quarter past six I was paying a hackie in front of the old brownstone and climbing out. As my foot touched the sidewalk, someone grabbed my arm and pronounced my name, and I wheeled.

It was Noel Tedder. "Who the hell does this Nero Wolfe think he is?" he squeaked.

"It depends on his mood." I moved my arm, but he had a grip. "Let go of my arm, I might need it. Why, did he bounce you?"

"I haven't been in. First I was told through a crack to come back after six, and I did. Then I was told Wolfe was busy—'engaged,' he said. I asked for you and was told you were out and he didn't know when you'd be back. I said I'd come in and wait, and he said I wouldn't. What does it take, a passport?"

"Did you give your name?"

"Certainly."

"Did you say what you want to see him about?"

"No. I'll tell him."

"Not unless you tell me first. Not only is that the routine, but also he's had a hard day. There was no homemade blackberry jam for breakfast, he had to skip his morning turn with the orchids, a police inspector came and annoyed him, and he had to read a long statement and sign it. If you tell me what you want, there may be a chance. If you don't, it's hopeless."

"Out here?"

"We can sit on the stoop if you'd rather."

He turned his head to look at a man and woman who were passing. He needed a shave. He also needed either a haircut, a comb and brush, or a hat, and his plaid jacket and striped slacks could have stood a little pressing. When the man and woman were ten paces away his eyes came back to me.

"I've got a chance to make a pot but I can't do it alone. I don't even know how to start. My mother told me that if I can find the money she paid the kidnapers, or any part of it, I can have it. Half a million. I want Wolfe to help me. He can have a fifth of it for his share."

My brows were up. "When did your mother tell you that?"

"Wednesday evening."

"She may feel different about it now."

"No, she doesn't. I asked her this afternoon. She's not very—she's in pretty bad shape—but I didn't think it would hurt to ask her. She said yes. She said she wouldn't want any of that money now anyhow."

My brows were still up. "The police know about the kidnaping. And the FBI."

"I don't know about the FBI. We told the police this morning."

"Dozens of trained men are on the job already. By tomorrow there'll be hundreds. Fat chance you'd have."

"Damn it, I know I wouldn't! That's why I've got to have Nero Wolfe! Isn't he better than they are?"

"That's a point." I was looking at another point. We had never taken a crack at that kind of problem, and if Wolfe could be peekayed into tackling it, it would be interesting to see how he went about it. It would also be interesting to collect his share if there was anything to share.

"I'll tell you," I said. "I doubt very much if Mr. Wolfe will touch it. He's not only eccentric, he hates to work, and he seldom takes a case on a contingent basis. But I'm willing to put it up to him. You may come inside to wait."

"If you can get inside," he squeaked. That tenor didn't fit his make-up at all.

"I can try," I said, and made for the stoop, and he followed me up. The chain-bolt was on, so I had to push the button. If Fritz, letting us in, was surprised to see me bringing a customer who had been turned away twice, he didn't show it. Fritz shows only what he thinks it is proper to show. I took Tedder to the front room and left him, and went to the office by way of the hall instead of the connecting door. Wolfe, at his desk, had the middle drawer open and was fingering in it. Counting caps of beer bottles to see how much he had gained on the week's quota by being away twenty-four hours. I waited to speak until he shut the drawer and looked up.

"Regards from Mandel. I didn't see the DA. They probably won't bother us again unless and until they have to decide that Jimmy Vail didn't die by accident, which they would hate to do. You have seen the *Gazette?*"

"Yes."

"Any comment?"

"No."

"Then I'm still not fired. I'm taking a leave of absence without pay. Say a month, but it may be more."

His lips tightened. He took a deep breath. "Are you bent on vexing me beyond endurance?"

"No, sir. I want to grab an opportunity. When I arrived just now Noel Tedder was there on the sidewalk, vexed beyond endurance because you wouldn't see him. His mother told him Wednesday that he could have the money she paid the kidnaper if he could find it and get it, and he came to offer you a one-fifth share to help him. Of course you wouldn't be interested now that you only take cases where all you have to do is put a notice in the paper, so I'm going to tell him I'll take it on myself. I took the liberty of putting him in the front room. I thought I ought to tell you first. Of course it's long odds, but if I got it, the whole pile, my cut would be a hundred grand and I could quit vexing you and open my own office, maybe with Saul Panzer for a partner, and we could—"

"Shut up."

"Yes, sir. That will be one advantage, you won't have to bellow—"

"Shut up."

"Yes, sir."

He regarded me, not with affection. "So you expect to badger me into this fantastic gamble."

"You might take a minute out to look at it. It would be satisfactory to find something that ten thousand cops and FBI men will be looking for. And each year when you top the eighty-per-cent bracket you relax. I admit it's a big if, but if you raked this in and added it to what you've already collected this year, you could relax until winter, and it's not May yet. If you missed, you would only be out expenses. As for my badgering you, we have nothing in prospect, and if I take a month off Fritz can dust your desk and empty the wastebasket and you can open the mail."

"That's bluster. You wouldn't."

"The hell I wouldn't."

He closed his eyes, probably to contemplate the rosy possibility of months and months with no work to do and no would-be customers admitted. In a minute he opened them and muttered, "Very well, bring him in."

7

As Noel Tedder sat in the red leather chair and crossed his legs, showing blue and yellow socks beneath the striped slacks. Wolfe surveyed him. He had to adjust to the outfit. I have heard him say that men who wear conventional clothes are sheep, but I have also heard him say that men who wear unconventional clothes are popinjays. You can't win.

Tedder asked him if I had told him what he wanted, and Wolfe nodded. He spoke. "The most unpromising enterprise I have ever been asked to undertake, if Mr. Goodwin understood you and I understood him. Mrs.

Vail, your mother, told you that if you recovered the money she paid to ransom her husband, you could keep it; and if I help you, you will pay me one-fifth of what we recover if we're successful, and nothing if we fail. Is that it?"

"That's it. Of course I—"

"If you please. When did your mother tell you that?"

"Wednesday evening. And again this afternoon. With Jimmy gone—my stepfather—I thought I'd better ask her."

"Wednesday evening, did she broach it or did you?"

" 'Broach'?"

"Bring it up. Introduce the idea."

"I don't remember. Does that matter?"

"It may. If you suggested it a conjecture enters. That you knew where the money was and you wanted to get it in a manner that would entitle you—don't interrupt—entitle you to keep it. You come to me for help because you can't very well just go and get it and produce it. You will give me hints, cannily of course, and guided by them Mr. Goodwin, under my direction, will find the money. Even if your hints have made me smell a rat, I'll hold my nose and take my share. So who broached it, your mother or you?"

Tedder tittered. I don't want to give a false impression, especially since I have mentioned his tenor. Men do titter. "Jesus," he said, "that would be pups. That would be sharp. But how would I know where it is?"

"You would know where you put it Tuesday night after you or your confederate took it from your mother on Iron Mine Road."

"Huh?" He was squinting. "You've lost me. Say it again."

Wolfe wiggled a finger. "Mr. Tedder. You have come to me with an extraordinary proposal, and naturally my first question is what about you? Did you kidnap your stepfather?"

"Balls. He might have recognized me."

"Did you have a hand in the kidnaping? Yes or no."

"No. N, O, no." Tedder was still squinting. "Got a Bible?"

"That wouldn't establish it. If I assume your good

faith, where are we? It would be witless to try to compete with the intricate and expert routine of the army of official investigators. If we start at all it must be from a point chosen by us and overlooked by them. Before I accept or decline your proposal I must know if you will agree with me on that point; and first of all I must ask, what if we find the money and your mother repudiates her engagement to let you keep it?"

"She won't."

"She might."

Tedder shook his head. "Four people besides me heard her say it—my sister Margot, her brother Ralph, Frost, the lawyer, and Jimmy. Of course Jimmy's dead."

"She still might. I must tell you that, if she does, my share will be legally collectible and I'll collect it."

"Sure, why not? You won't have to. My mother won't renege. What's the point I have to agree on?"

"It's a series of assumptions, and you may not like them. The first and basic one is that Mr. Vail's death was not an accident. He was murdered."

"Huh?" Tedder uncrossed his legs and sat up. "He pulled that goddam statue over on him."

"No." Wolfe was emphatic. "I concede that that's conceivable; it may even be sufficiently plausible for the police to accept it; but I reject it. There is no implication in the published accounts that he was drunk. Was he?"

"No."

"Had he been drinking?"

"He had had a couple, not more. His usual, bourbon and water. He could handle half a dozen. He wasn't even started. He was just sleepy. He said he couldn't keep his eyes open and went to the couch."

"And later, after you and the others had gone— Did you turn the lights off when you left?"

"All but one. Mother said to leave one on."

"A good light?"

"Fairly good. A floor lamp by the wall."

"And he awoke enough to realize where he was, leave the couch, stand, and walk; and, losing his balance, he caught at the statue, which was insecure, and brought it down on him. It's possible, but I don't believe it. I do not believe that a man awake enough to walk would be so befuddled that he couldn't dodge a falling statue. Was it on a direct line from the couch to the door?"

"Not direct, but not far out." Tedder was squinting again. "You said murder. How? Was he so sound asleep that he didn't wake up when someone dragged him off the couch and over to the statue and pushed it over on him? Do you believe that?"

"No. He was drugged."

"The hell he was."

"He must have been. In one of his drinks. The handiest assumption is chloral hydrate, which is easily procured. In solution in an alcoholic beverage it has almost no taste. A moderate dose induces a deep sleep approaching coma. It decomposes rapidly and will not be detected by an autopsy unless it is performed within three or four hours after death, and even then the only reliable test is identification of urochloralic acid in the urine. That test is made only when chloral hydrate is specifically suspected, and with Mr. Vail I doubt if it was. I am not parading; I had this surmise yesterday and consulted a book."

He hadn't mentioned it to me; it would have been admitting that Jimmy Vail's death might possibly be of interest to us. We had several books on toxicology on the shelves, but he hadn't been here yesterday, so he must have found one when he was going over Doc Vollmer's shelves. I had had personal experience of chloral hydrate, having once been served a Mickey Finn by a woman named Dora Chapin. Two hours after I had swallowed it you could have rowed me out to Bedloe's Island and pushed the Statue of Liberty onto me and I wouldn't have batted an eye.

Wolfe was going on. "So that Mr. Vail was murdered with deliberation may properly be called a deduction, not an assumption. Not a final deduction, but a basic one, for it is the ground for my assumptions. Whether you like it or not, do you concur?"

"I don't know." Tedder's tongue showed between his lips. "Go on with your assumptions."

"They're purely tentative, to establish a starting point. But first another deduction, made three days ago, on Tuesday, by Mr. Goodwin and me. Dinah Utley, your mother's secretary, was implicated in the kidnaping, and not indirectly or passively. She had an active hand in it. Her death—"

"How do you know that?"

"By observed evidence and interpretation of it. I'll reserve it. I'm exposing my position, Mr. Tedder, because I have to if you're going to occupy it with me, but I need not reveal all the steps that have led to it. I'm taking your good faith as a working hypothesis, but there is still that conjecture—that you had a part in the kidnaping and you know where the money is. If so, it was an egregious blunder to come to me. I'll get my share of the money, and you'll get your share of doom. Do you want to withdraw before I commit myself to this mad gamble? Do you want to leave?"

"Hell no. You talk a lot and you talk big."

"I hope to the point—our starting point. I am almost there. Miss Utley was involved in the kidnaping and was murdered. Mr. Vail was the victim of the kidnaping and was murdered. My assumptions are, first, that both murders were consequential to the kidnaping operation; and second, that the person who killed Mr. Vail, with premeditation since he drugged him, being involved in the kidnaping, knows where the money is. He was present at the gathering at that house Wednesday evening. Therefore, if we are to find the money, our starting point is that house and its occupants. If you will proceed from that point with me, I'll accept your proposal."

Tedder was chewing his lips. "Jesus," he said. He chewed some more. "The way you put it . . . I guess I'm in over my head. You're saying one of them killed Jimmy —Uncle Ralph or Frost or my sister."

"Or your mother or you."

"Sure, we were there." He shook his head. "Holy Christ. My mother, that's crazy. Me, I liked Jimmy. He couldn't see me, but I liked him. Uncle Ralph—"

"That's irrelevant, Mr. Tedder. The murder resulted from the kidnaping—my assumption. The kidnaper wished him no harm and rendered him none; he only wanted the money. Logically that excludes your mother, but not you. There are several possibilities. For one, Miss Utley was killed because she demanded too large a share of the loot. For another, Mr. Vail was killed because he had learned that one of those present Wednesday evening was responsible for the kidnaping, and of course that wouldn't do. We ignore the mysterious Mr. Knapp perforce, because we don't know who or where he is. Presumably he was a confederate whose chief function was to make the phone calls, but he may also have got the money from your mother, since he spoke to her, and if he has bolted with it, we're done before we start. We could expose the murderer, to no profit, but that's all. I say 'we.' Is it 'we'? Do we proceed?"

"How?"

"First I would need to speak at length, separately, with those who were present Wednesday evening, beginning with you. You would have to bring them here, or send them, by some pretext—or some inducement, perhaps a share of the money. Then I'll see."

"Great. Just great. I ask them—my sister, for instance—to come and let you grill her to find out if she kidnaped Jimmy and then killed him. Great."

"You might manage to put it more tactfully."

"Yeah, I might." He leaned forward. "Look, Mr. Wolfe. Maybe you've got it right, your deductions and assumptions, and maybe not. If you have and you find the money, okay, I'll get mine and you'll get yours. I don't owe my uncle a damn thing, and God knows I don't owe that lawyer, Andrew Frost, anything. He talked my mother out of letting me have—oh, to hell with it. As for my sister, I'm not her keeper, repeat not—she can look out for herself. You try putting it to her tactfully and see what—"

The phone rang. I swiveled and got it. "Nero Wolfe's residence, Archie Goodwin speaking."

"This is Margot Tedder. I'd like to speak to Mr. Wolfe."

I told her to hold it and turned. "Margot Tedder wants to speak to you."

Noel made a noise. Wolfe frowned at his phone to remind it that he resents being summoned by it, no matter who, then reached for it. "Yes, Miss Tedder?"

"Nero Wolfe?"

"Yes."

"You never go anywhere, do you?"

"No."

"Then I'll have to come there. I'll come now."

"You won't be admitted. I'll be at dinner. Why do you wish to come?"

"I want you to help me do something."

"What?"

"I'd rather— Oh, it doesn't matter. About the money my mother gave the kidnapers. You know about that."

"Yes. What about it?"

"She has told me that if I can find it I can have it, and I want you to help me. We'll have to hurry. I'll come now. Your dinner can wait."

"I can't. More precisely, I won't. You may come at nine o'clock, not before. I'm busy. You will excuse me. I'm hanging up." He cradled the phone and turned. "Your sister says that her mother told her that if she finds the money paid to the kidnaper she can have it, and she is coming at nine o'clock to enlist my help. I'll tell her you have already engaged me. We have twenty minutes until my dinnertime. Where were you from eight o'clock Sunday evening until eight o'clock Wednesday morning?"

8

A man's time-and-place record as given by him may or may not prove anything, even if it doesn't check. There are a lot of people who wouldn't tell you exactly where* they had been and what they had done between eight p.m. Sunday and eight a.m. Wednesday even if they hadn't kidnaped or murdered anybody. Wolfe, knowing how easy it is to frame an alibi, has seldom tried to crack one. In all the years I have been with him I haven't checked more than four or five. He has sometimes had Saul Panzer or Fred Durkin or Orrie Cather look into one, but not often. I put what Noel Tedder told him in my notebook, but I knew it wouldn't be checked unless developments nominated Noel for the tag. Besides, only one time and place was essential, either for Noel or for one of the others. It didn't have to be that he himself had snatched Jimmy Vail Sunday evening, or had helped to keep him wherever he had been kept, or had put notes in telephone books Tuesday evening, or had been at Iron Mine Road Tuesday night. The one essential time and place was the Harold F. Tedder library Wednesday evening, and we knew he had been there. They all had. The question had to be asked; if Noel had gone up in a balloon with six United States Senators Sunday morning and hadn't come down until Wednesday noon, he couldn't be expected to know where the money was, and that was the point. But I won't waste my space and your time reporting his whereabouts for those sixty hours.

More interesting was his reaction to the news that Margot was coming to see Wolfe. It fussed him more than anything Wolfe had said to him. When he said he didn't believe his mother had told her that, he had to squeeze it through his teeth. Evidently he had some strong feeling about his sister, and it wasn't brotherly love. Wolfe tried to ask him questions about Dinah Utley and her relations with Purcell and Frost and Margot, but got no usable answers. Noel wanted to be damn sure that Wolfe wasn't going to let Margot talk him into switching to her. He even offered to bring Uncle Ralph that evening and Andrew Frost in the morning. When Fritz announced dinner he followed Wolfe to the dining-room door, and I had to take his arm and start him to the front.

Returning and entering the dining room, I found that Wolfe had pulled his chair out but hadn't sat. "A grotesque venture," he grunted. "Preposterous. Will that woman be punctual?"

"Probably not." I pulled my chair back. "She's not the punctual type."

"But she may be. You'll have to be at the phone with your coffee to get Saul and Fred and Orrie. In my room in the morning at eight, and in the office with you at nine." Fritz was there with the stuffed clams, and he sat and took the spoon and fork. He couldn't have sat before giving me instructions because that would have been talking business during a meal, and by heck a rule is a rule is a rule. As I helped myself to clams I held my breath because if you smell them, mixed with shallots, chives, chervil, mushrooms, bread crumbs, sherry, and dry white wine, you take so many that you don't leave enough room for the duckling roasted in cider with Spanish sauce as revised by Wolfe and Fritz, leaving out the carrot and parsley and putting anchovies in. As I ate the clams I remarked to myself that we darned well had better find at least some leavings of the half a million, since Saul and Fred and Orrie came to twenty-five bucks an hour, plus expenses.

I don't know how Wolfe first got the notion that when I've had one good look at a woman and heard her speak, especially if she's under thirty, I can answer any question he wants to ask about her, but I know he still has it, chiefly on account of little items like my saying that Margot Tedder wouldn't be punctual. She was twenty-five minutes late. Of course if she had been on time I would have commented that she must need some ready cash quick. When you once get a reputation, or it gets you, you're stuck with it for good.

I have said that from hearsay she kept her chin up so she could look down her nose, and her manners when she entered the old brownstone didn't contradict it. Crossing the threshold, she gave me a nod for a butler, though I hadn't seen one at 994 Fifth Avenue, and when I took her to the office she stopped at the edge of the big rug, looked it over from side to side and end to end, and asked Wolfe, "Is that a Kazak?"

"No," he said. "Shirvan."

"You can't possibly appreciate it. Is it yours?"

"I doubt it. It was given to me in nineteen thirty-two, in Cairo, by a man to whom I had rendered a service, and I suspected he had stolen it in Kandahar. If it wasn't rightfully his, it isn't rightfully mine. But of course illegality of ownership does not extend indefinitely. If my possession of that rug were challenged by an heir of the Kandahar prince who once owned it, or by one of his wives or concubines, I would enter a defense. It would be a borderline case. After sufficient time legal ownership is undisputed. Your grandfather was a bandit; some of his forays were almost certainly actionable. But if a descendant of one of his victims tried to claim that fur thing you are wearing, she would be laughed at. I'm pleased that you recognize the quality of the rug, though only an ignoramus could mistake it for a Kazak. Kazaks have a long pile. You are Margot Tedder? I am Nero Wolfe." He pointed to the red leather chair. "Sit down and tell me what you want."

She had opened her mouth a couple of times to cut in on him, but Wolfe in full voice is not easy to interrupt, particularly if his eyes are pinning you. "I told you on the phone what I want," she said.

"You will please sit down, Miss Tedder. I like eyes at a level."

She glanced at me. The poor girl was stuck. She didn't want to sit down because he had ordered her to, but to stay on her feet would be silly. She compromised. One of the yellow chairs was at the end of my desk, and she came and sat on it. As I have said, when she walked you might have thought her hips were in a cast, but sitting she wasn't at all hard to look at.

"I didn't come," she said, "to listen to a lecture about legal ownership by a detective. You know what I came for. My mother paid you sixty thousand dollars for nothing. All you did was put that thing in the paper. For sixty thousand dollars you certainly ought to help me find the money my mother gave the kidnaper. That's more than ten per cent."

Wolfe grunted. "Twelve. That might be thought adequate. How would I go about it? Have you a suggestion?"

"Of course not. You would go about it the way any detective would. That's your business."

"Could I count on your cooperation?"

She frowned at him, her chin up. "How could I cooperate?"

He didn't frown back. Having put her in her place, he didn't mind if she didn't stay put. "That would depend on developments," he said. "Take a hypothesis. Do you know what a hypothesis is?"

"You're being impertinent."

"Not without provocation. You didn't know what a Shirvan is. The hypothesis: If I took the job you offer, I would want to begin by asking you some questions. For example, what were your relations with Dinah Utley?"

She stared. "What on earth has that got to do with finding the money?"

He nodded. "I thought so. You're under a misapprehension. You expected me to pit my wits and Mr. Goodwin's eyes and legs against the horde of official investigators who are combing the countryside and looking under every stone. Pfui. That would be infantile. I would have to approach it differently, and the best way—indeed, the only way—would be through Dinah Utley. You know that Mr. Goodwin and I suspected that she was implicated in the kidnaping; you heard your mother and Mr. Goodwin discuss it Wednesday afternoon. Now we don't suspect it; we know it. Therefore—"

"How do you know it? Because she was there and was killed?"

"Partly that, but there were other factors. She was here Tuesday afternoon. Therefore at least one of the kidnapers was someone with whom she had had contacts, and I would want to learn all I could about her. How well did you know her?"

"Why—she was my mother's secretary. She lived in the house, but she didn't regard herself as a servant. I thought my mother let her take too many liberties."

"What kind of liberties?"

"Different kinds. She ate with us. If we had people in for cocktails, she came in if she felt like it. If I asked her to do something, she might and she might not. You might have thought we were equals. You know, I must say, I think this is clever. Perhaps you *are* clever. I should have thought of this myself, about Dinah, only I really don't know much about her. She was there seven years, and I suppose she had friends of her own class, but I never saw them."

"Would your brother know more about her?"

"He might." She nodded. "Yes, I'm sure he would. He did things with her just to irritate me—like playing cards with her. Gin rummy in the library. You might have thought *they* were equals, and perhaps they should have been. Once he took her to a prizefight."

"That sounds promising. I would want to talk with him. I don't want to shock you, Miss Tedder, but the question should be asked. Is it conceivable that the kidnaping was a joint enterprise of Miss Utley and your brother? That your brother had a hand in it?"

"Good heavens." Her lips parted. She stared. "Of course

it's conceivable. That's the second thing you've thought of that *I* should have thought of."

"Given time, undoubtedly you would have. Your emotions have interfered with your mental processes. We would—"

"But if he—Noel—then he knows where the money is! He *has* the money?"

"Not too fast, Miss Tedder. That's merely a surmise. We would have to consider all possibilities, all those who had frequent opportunity to see Miss Utley. I understand that your mother's brother, Ralph Purcell, lives in that house. Was he on good terms with her?"

She was only half listening. He had darned near lost her with his suggestion about Noel. I wouldn't have been surprised if she had bounced up, granting that a person of her class and with her hips could bounce, and gone to have it out with her brother. Wolfe saw he would have to repeat his question, and did so.

"Oh," she said, "he's on good terms with everybody, or he tries to be. He ran errands for Dinah, but of course he would. He runs errands for me too. He's all right, I like him, I really do, but he's so—oh, well. He just doesn't belong. He certainly wouldn't have anything to do with any kidnaping; he wouldn't have the nerve."

"But he was friendly enough with Miss Utley to make it plausible that he knows the names of her associates not of your class, and possibly has met some of them."

"Yes. No doubt of that. You won't have to talk with my brother. I'll talk with him."

"That would help. That was the sort of thing I had in mind when I asked if I could count on your cooperation. I believe I have named all those who had— No, there's another possibility. I saw in the newspaper the name of your mother's attorney—Frost, I think?"

"Yes. Andrew Frost."

"It might be that an attorney would have frequent contacts with a client's secretary, especially if he is also the client's business adviser. Did Mr. Frost see much of Miss Utley?"

"I suppose he did, but I don't know, after she came to work for my mother. Of course he saw her when she worked for him. She was his secretary. He let my mother take her. It was supposed to be a great favor, but he really did it for my father. My father died not long after that. My father was a true gentleman. I'd like to tell you something, I don't know why, if you'll promise not to repeat it. Do you promise?"

"Yes."

Her eyes came to me. "Do you?"

"Sure."

She went back to Wolfe. "My father told me once that his father was a bandit."

There you are. She was actually human.

Wolfe nodded. "Then I merely corroborated him. I am obliged to you, Miss Tedder. Manifestly, if I took the job you offer, I would need to speak with Mr. Purcell and Mr. Frost. I would also need to be informed about the gathering in the library of your home Wednesday evening. For example, I understand that drinks were served. Who served them?"

She frowned again. "Why? Why do you need to know that?"

"You conceded the possibility that I am clever. Any discussion in which Mr. Purcell and Mr. Frost and your brother took part may be informative. You say that Mr. Purcell likes to do errands. Did he serve the drinks?"

"No. The bar cart was there and we served ourselves, or someone—you know how it is. I think—yes, Uncle Ralph took brandy to Mr. Frost. My mother likes a champagne cobbler after dinner, and she mixes it herself. She poured me some champagne, but I didn't drink much."

"What did your brother have?"

"Champagne. He gulps it."

"And Mr. Vail?"

"I didn't notice, but probably bourbon and water. No matter how clever you are, this can't possibly mean anything. You're just trying to impress me." She glanced at her wristwatch. "Do you want to see my uncle first? He would come tonight if I tell him to."

"Not tonight." Wolfe cocked his head. "I'm not trying to impress you, but I have imposed on you. I must reject your demand, Miss Tedder—I shouldn't have called it an offer, since you have offered nothing. Your brother has.

He was here this afternoon, and I have engaged with him to recover the money. My share will be one-fifth."

She was gawking. Of course a person of her class shouldn't gawk, but you can't blame her. A person of my class would have thrown something at him. "You're lying," she said. "You're trying to make me say you can have part of it. Of course one-fifth would be ridiculous. You already have more than enough from my mother, but I suppose, if you—very well, if you get it I'll give you ten thousand dollars. If you get *all* of it. Of course you'll have to do it, after everything I've told you."

Wolfe was slowly moving his head from side to side. "Amazing," he said. "How old are you?"

"I'm not a minor, if that's what you're thinking. I'm twenty-one."

"Amazing that a creature so obtuse could live so long without meeting disaster. I was at pains to make it clear that we were discussing a hypothesis, and the idea that you were being gulled never entered your mind. I don't know how a brain that is never used passes the time. It will be futile to try to browbeat your brother into deferring to you; I shall hold him to his engagement with me. I was not lying when I said that he anticipated you. He was here when you telephoned."

I suppose her father, Harold F. Tedder, was responsible for the way she took it. Naturally a true gentleman would teach his children never to argue with underlings. Since she couldn't very well order him to leave, his office and his house, there was only one thing to do, and she did it. She got up and walked out, stiff hips and all. She did it all right, too, no hurry and no prolonging it. I got to the hall ahead of her and had the door open when she reached the front, and she said thank you as she passed. Breeding will tell. I shut the door, bolted it for the night, returned to the office, and told Wolfe, "Taking candy from a baby."

He grunted and pushed his chair back. "An insupportable day. I'm going to my bed." He rose.

"What about Saul and Fred and Orrie?"

"The morning will do." He moved.

9

Saturday morning I heard the seven-o'clock news on the radio in my room, and the eight-o'clock news on the radio in the kitchen. Saul and Fred and Orrie had come and had gone up to Wolfe's room. I was listening to the nine-o'clock news on the radio in the office when they came down. Ordinarily two or three times a day is often enough, but ordinarily I am not curious as to whether some dick or state cop or FBI hero has found half a million bucks, with or without a Mr. Knapp in illegal possession of it.

I had also read the morning paper. The DA's office was playing it safe on the death of Jimmy Vail. The cause of death had been Benjamin Franklin, definitely, and there was no evidence or information to indicate that it had not been an accident, but it was still under investigation. I doubted that last. The DA had to say it, to guard against the chance of something popping up, but I doubted if the five people who had last seem him alive were being pestered much.

There was no doubt at all that the kidnaping was being investigated. Since Jimmy had died before telling anyone how or where he had been snatched, or where and by whom he had been kept, or where he had been released, there was no lead at all. The caretaker of the country house near Katonah had been taken apart by a dozen experts, but he had stuck to it that Vail had left in his Thunderbird shortly after eight Sunday evening to drive back to town, and had returned in the Thunderbird about half past seven Wednesday morning, tired, mad, dirty, and hungry. He had told the caretaker nothing whatever. The theory was that the kidnapers had taken the Thunderbird and kept it wherever they had kept him, and, when they turned him loose, had let him have it to drive home in, which was a perfectly good theory, since they certainly wouldn't want to use it. It was being examined by a task force of scientists, for fingerprints, of course, and for where and how far it had been, and who and what had been in it. It was described both in the paper and on the radio, and shown on television, with the request that anyone who had seen it between Sunday evening and Wednesday morning should communicate immediately with the police, the Westchester DA, or the FBI.

Also described, but not shown on television, was the suitcase the money had been in: tan leather, 28 by 16 by 9, old and stained, scuffed a little, three brass clasps, one in the middle and one near each end. Mrs. Vail had taken it to the bank, where the money had been put in it, and the description had been supplied by the bank's vice-president. It was the property of Jimmy Vail—or had been.

The best prospect of some kind of a lead was finding someone who had been at Fowler's Inn or The Fatted Calf Tuesday evening and had seen one of the kidnapers. The man Mrs. Vail had given the suitcase to had had his face covered. It was assumed that a confederate had been present at both places to make sure that Mrs. Vail didn't show anyone the notes she got from the phone books. People at both places remembered seeing Mrs. Vail, and the cashier at Fowler's Inn had seen her go to the phone book and open it, but no one had been found who had seen anybody take a visible interest in her.

Funeral services for Jimmy Vail would be held at the Dunstan Chapel Saturday morning at eleven.

Thanks to Nero Wolfe and Archie Goodwin, though no one but Lon Cohen was thanking us, the murder of Dinah Utley was getting a big play both in print and on the air. Not only had her body been found at or near the spot where Mrs. Vail had delivered the suitcase, but also someone had leaked it, either in White Plains or in Manhattan, that she had been an accomplice in the kidnaping. So Cramer had bought the deduction Wolfe had made from the notes and had passed it on to Westchester, and when Ben Dykes came at eleven-thirty there would be some fancy explaining to do.

As I said, I was in the office listening to the nine-o'clock news when Saul and Fred and Orrie came down from Wolfe's room. The kidnaping and murder items had been covered, so I switched it off and greeted them. If you wanted an operative for a tough job and were offered your pick of those three, never having seen or heard of them before, you would probably take Fred Durkin or Orrie Cather, and you would be wrong. Fred was big and broad, and looked solid and honest and was, but from the neck up he was a little too solid for situations that needed quick reactions. Orrie was tall and handsome and smart, and in any situation his reaction was speedy enough, but it might be the right reaction and it might not. Saul was small and wiry, with a long narrow face and a big nose. He always looked as if he would need a shave in another hour, he wore a cap instead of a hat, and his pants had always been pressed a week ago. But there wasn't an agency in New York that wouldn't have taken him on at the top figure if he hadn't preferred to free lance, and at ten dollars an hour he was a bargain for any job you could name.

"Six hundred three ways," Orrie said. "And I want a picture of Noel Tedder."

"I'll take one of Ralph Purcell," Fred said.

"So you're taking one apiece?" I went to the safe and squatted to twirl the knob. "The very best way to waste time and money. Foolproof. As for pictures, I only have newspaper shots."

"I'll get them from Lon," Saul said. "Mr. Wolfe says your credit's good with him."

"It sure is." I swung the safe door open and got the cash box. "Credit, hell. A truckload of pictures wouldn't make a dent in what he owes us. So you've got Andrew Frost?"

He said he had, and added that Wolfe had said that I would be in the office to receive reports. I had known that was coming. In a tough case it's nice to know that we have three good men on the job, even for chores as chancy as solo tailing, but the catch is that I have to sit there on the back of my lap to answer the phone and go to help if needed. I gave each of them two cees in used fives, tens, and twenties, made entries in the cash book, and supplied a few routine details, and they went. They had arrived at eight and it was then nine-thirty, so we were already out $37.50.

I was behind on the germination and blooming records, which I typed on cards from notes Wolfe brought down from the plant rooms, so after opening the mail I got the drawer from the cabinet and began entering items like "27 flks agar slp no fung sol B autoclaved 18 lbs 4/18/61." I was fully expecting a phone call from either Noel or Margot, or possibly their mother, but none had come by eleven, when Wolfe came down. There would be no calls now, since they would all be at the funeral services.

The session with Ben Dykes, who came at 11:40, ten minutes late, which I had thought would be fairly ticklish, wasn't bad at all. He didn't even hint at any peril to us, as far as he was concerned, though he mentioned that Hobart was considering whether we should be summoned and charged. What he wanted was information. He had seen our signed statement, and he knew what he had told Cramer and I had told Mandel, but he wanted more. So he laid off. Though he didn't say so, for him the point was that a kidnaper had collected half a million dollars right there in his county, and there was a chance that it was still in his county, stashed somewhere, and finding it would give him a lot of pleasure, not to mention profit. If at the same time he got a line on the murderer of Dinah Utley, okay, but that wasn't the main point. So he stayed for more than an hour, trying to find a crumb, some little thing that Mrs. Vail or Dinah Utley or Jimmy had said that might give him a trace of a scrap of a hint. When, going to the hall with him to let him out, I said Westchester was his and he and his men must know their way around, he said yeah, but the problem was to keep from being jostled or tramped on by the swarms of state cops and FBI supermen.

At one o'clock the radio had nothing new, and neither had we. Saul and Fred and Orrie had phoned in. They had all gone to the funeral, which was a big help. That's one of the fine features of tailing; wherever the subject leads you, you will follow. I once spent four hours tagging a guy up and down Fifth and Madison Avenues, using all the tricks and dodges I knew, and learned later that he had been trying to find a pair of gray suspenders with a yellow stripe.

It was one of those days. Shad roe again for lunch, this time larded with pork and baked in cream with an assortment of herbs. Every spring I get so fed up with shad roe that I wish to heaven fish would figure out some other way. Whales have. Around three o'clock, when we were back in the office, there was a development, if you don't care what you call it. The phone rang and it was Orrie Cather. He said his and Fred's subjects were together, so they were. He was in a booth at 54th and Lexington. Noel Tedder and Ralph Purcell had just entered a drugstore across the street. That was all. Ten seconds after I hung up it rang again. Noel Tedder. You couldn't beat that for a thrill to make your spine tingle: Fred and Orrie across the street, eagle-eyed, and the subject talking to me on the phone. He said he had persuaded Purcell to come and talk with Wolfe and he would be here in twenty minutes. I turned and asked Wolfe, and he looked at the clock and said of course not, and I turned back to the phone.

"Sorry, Mr. Tedder, Mr. Wolfe will be—"

"I knew it! My sister!"

"Not your sister. He turned her down, and the arrangement with you stands. But he'll be busy from four to six. Can Mr. Purcell come at six?"

"I'll see. Hold the wire." In half a minute: "Yes, he'll be there at six o'clock."

"Good." I hung up and swiveled. "Six o'clock. Wouldn't it be amusing if he gives us a hot lead and Fred and I hop on it—of course Fred will tail him here and be out front—and we're two hours late getting there and someone already has it? Just a lousy two hours."

Wolfe grunted. "You know quite well that if I permit exceptions to my schedule I soon will have no schedule. You would see to that."

I could have made at least a dozen comments, but what was the use? I turned to the typewriter and the cards. When he left for the plant rooms at 3:59 I turned on the radio. Nothing new. Again at five o'clock. Nothing new. When the *Gazette* came it had pictures of fourteen people who had been at Fowler's Inn or The Fatted Calf Tuesday evening, which showed what a newspaper that's on its toes can do to keep the public informed. I was back at the typewriter when the doorbell rang at 5:55. I went to the hall, saw Ralph Purcell through the one-way glass, and stepped to the door and opened it, and he said apologetically, "I guess I'm a little early," and offered a hand. I took it. What the hell, it wouldn't be the first murderer I had shaken hands with.

As I took his hat the elevator jolted to a stop at the bottom, the door opened, and Wolfe emerged, three minutes ahead of time because he likes to be in his chair when company comes.

Purcell went to him. "I'm Ralph Purcell, Mr. Wolfe." He had a hand out. "I'm a great admirer of yours. I'm Mrs. Jimmy Vail's brother."

Of course Wolfe had to take the hand, and when he does take a hand, which is seldom, he really takes it. As we went to the office Purcell was wiggling his fingers. Wolfe told him to take the red leather chair, went to his, got his bulk arranged, and spoke.

"I assume Mr. Tedder has explained the situation to you?"

Purcell was looking at me. When I gave Wolfe a report I am supposed to include everything, and I usually do, and I had had all the time there was Thursday afternoon at Doc Vollmer's, but I had left out an item about Purcell. I had described him, of course—round face like his sister's, a little pudgy, going bald—but I had neglected to mention that when someone started to say something he looked at someone else. I now learned that he didn't go so far as to look at A when he was speaking to B. His eyes went to Wolfe.

"Yes," he said, "Noel explained it, but I'm not sure—it seems a little—"

"Perhaps I can elucidate it. What did he say?"

"He said you were going to find the money for him— the money my sister paid the kidnaper. He asked me if I remembered that my sister had told him he could have the money if he found it, and of course I did. Then it seemed to be a little confused, but maybe it was just confused in my mind. Something about you wanted to ask me some questions because you thought one of us might know something about it on account of Dinah, Dinah Utley, and I thought he said something about one of us putting something in Jimmy's drink, but when I asked about it he said you would explain that part of it."

So Noel had been fairly tactful after all, at least with Uncle Ralph.

Wolfe nodded. "It's a little complicated. The best— Why do you look at Mr. Goodwin when I speak?"

As Purcell's eyes left me a flush came to his cheeks. "It's a habit," he said, "a very bad habit."

"It is indeed."

"I know. You notice my eyes stick out?"

"Not flagrantly.

"Thank you, but they do. When I was a boy people said I stared. One person especially. She—" He stopped abruptly. In a moment he went on. "That was long ago, but that's why I do it. I only do it when someone starts speaking. After I talk a little I'm all right. I'm all right now."

"Then I'll proceed." Wolfe propped his elbows on the chair arms and joined his fingertips to make a tent. "You know that Miss Utley had a hand in the kidnaping."

"No, sir, I don't. I mean I don't know it, and I guess I don't believe it. I heard what my sister said to Mr. Goodwin and what he said to her, and that's all I know. The reason I don't believe it, kidnaping is so dangerous, if you get caught you don't stand any chance, and Dinah wasn't like that. She wasn't one to take big chances. I know that from how she played cards. Gin. She would hang onto a card she couldn't possibly use if she thought it might fill me. Of course everyone does that if you know it will, but she did it if she only thought it might. You see?"

Wolfe didn't, since he never plays cards, gin or anything else, but he nodded. "But you do take chances?"

"Oh, yes, I'm a born gambler. Three times my sister has staked me to some kind of wild idea I had—no, four —and none of them panned out. I'll bet on anything. When I have anything to bet with."

"Life needs some seasoning," Wolfe conceded. "As for Miss Utley, you are wrong. She was involved in the kidnaping. If I told you how that has been established to my satisfaction you would probably still be skeptical. But having come to indulge Mr. Tedder, now that you're here you might as well indulge me. If Miss Utley was involved, at least one of the kidnapers is someone she knew, and therefore I want information about her friends and acquaintances. I suppose you know them, some of them?"

"Well." Purcell shifted his weight in the chair. "Now, that's funny. Dinah's friends. Of course she had friends, she must have, but I don't really *know* any. She often went out evenings, movies and shows and so on, but I don't know who she went with. That's funny. I thought I knew her pretty well. Of course for acquaintances, she met a lot of people—"

The phone rang. I took it and got a familiar voice. "Archie? Fred. In a booth at the corner. Do I snatch a bite and come back or do I call it a day? I'm supposed to stay on him till he goes home. How long will he be there?"

"Hold it." I turned to Wolfe. "Fred. His subject has entered a building, a tumble-down dump that could be a den of vice. He wants instructions. Should he crash it?"

Wolfe shot me a mean glance. "Tell him to quit for the day and resume in the morning." To Purcell: "You were saying?"

But Uncle Ralph waited until I had relayed the order, hung up, and swiveled. Good manners, even if he didn't belong. "About Dinah's acquaintances," he said, "she met a lot of people there at the house, dinner guests and now and then a party, but that wouldn't be what you want. You want a different type, someone she might use for something dangerous like kidnaping."

"Or someone who might use her."

Purcell shook his head. "No, sir. I don't think Dinah would take a chance at kidnaping, but if she did she would be in charge. She would be the boss." He lifted a hand for a gesture. "I said I'm an admirer of yours, Mr. Wolfe, and I really mean it. A great admirer. I know you're never wrong about anything, and if you're sure Dinah was involved you must have a good reason. I thought I knew her pretty well, and naturally I'm curious, but of course if you're not telling anyone . . ."

"I have told someone." Wolfe regarded him. "I have told the police, and it will probably soon be public knowledge, so I may as well satisfy your curiosity. Miss Utley typed the notes—the one that your sister received in the mail and the two she found in the telephone books. Indubitably."

No perceptible reaction. You might have thought Purcell hadn't heard. The only muscles that moved were the ones that blinked his eyelids as he kept focused on Wolfe Then he said, "Thank you for telling me. That shows I'm not as big a ninny as some people think I am. I suspected something like that when they asked me if I knew who had taken the typewriter from my sister's study."

"The police asked you?"

"Yes. I didn't tell them, because I— Well, I didn't, but I'll tell you. I saw Dinah take it. Tuesday evening. Her car was parked in front, her own car, and I saw her take the typewriter out of the house, so she must have put it in the car."

"What time Tuesday evening?"

"I didn't notice, but it was before nine o'clock. It was about an hour after my sister had left in her car with the suitcase in it."

"How did you know the suitcase was in it?"

"I carried it out for her and put it in the trunk. I saw her with it upstairs and offered to take it. She didn't tell me where she was going, and I didn't ask her. I thought something was wrong, but I didn't know what. I thought she was probably going wherever Jimmy was. He had been gone since Sunday, and I didn't think he was at Katonah, and my sister hadn't told us where he was." Purcell shook his head. "So Dinah typed the notes, and so she took the typewriter. I've got to thank you for telling me. So you're right about her, and I thought I knew her. You know, I was playing gin with her a week ago Thursday—no, Friday—and of course she had it all planned then. That's hard to believe, but I guess I've got to believe it, and I can see why you want to know about her friends. If I could tell you I would. Is it all right to tell my sister about her typing the notes?"

"Your sister has probably already been told by the police." Wolfe palmed the chair arms. "You haven't been much help, Mr. Purcell, but you have been candid, and I appreciate it. Mr. Tedder should thank you, and no doubt he will. I needn't keep you any longer."

"But you were going to explain about someone putting something in Jimmy's drink."

"So I was. Wednesday evening in the library. You were there."

"Yes."

"You served brandy to Mr. Frost."

"Yes, I believe I did. How did— Oh, Noel told you."

"No, his sister told me. I had the idea of trying to get from her who could, and who could not, have drugged Mr. Vail's drink, but abandoned it. Such an inquiry is nearly always futile; memories are too faulty and interests too tangled. The point is simple: Mr. Vail must have been drugged when he was pulled off the couch and across to the statue, therefore someone put something in his drink. That's the explanation."

The reaction to that was perceptible. Purcell stared, not blinking. "Pulled?" he asked. "You said pulled?"

"Yes."

"But he wasn't *pulled*. Unless you mean he pulled himself."

"No. He was unconscious. Someone pulled him across to the statue, to the desired spot, and pushed the statue over on him. I'm not going to elaborate on that, not now, to you; I mentioned it only because I felt I owed you an explanation of Mr. Tedder's remark about Mr. Vail's drink."

"But you're saying Jimmy was murdered."

"Yes."

"But the police don't say he was."

"No?"

"But you didn't tell Noel that."

"But I did."

"You told Noel Jimmy was murdered?"

"Yes."

"You don't know that. You can't."

"The word 'know' has various connotations. I have formed that conclusion."

"Then you didn't really—you don't care about Dinah Utley. You've been taking advantage of me." His cheeks were red. "You've been making a fool of me." He got to his feet. "Noel should have told me. That wasn't fair.

You should have told me too. I guess I *am* a fool." He turned and headed for the door.

I stayed in my chair. There are times when it's better to let a departing guest get his own hat and open the door for himself. When I heard it close I went to the hall to see that he had remembered to cross the sill before he shut it, then went back to my desk. Wolfe had straightened up and was making faces.

"If he's it," I said, "if he's *not* a fool, you might as well cross it off."

He made another face.

10

I have never completely understood Wolfe's attitude on food and eating and probably never will. In some ways it's strictly personal. If Fritz presents a platter of broiled squabs and one of them is a little plumper or a more beautiful brown than the others, Wolfe cops it. If the supply of wild thyme honey from Greece is getting low, I am given to understand, through Fritz, that plain American honey on griddle cakes is quite acceptable. And so on. But it really pains him if I am out on a prolonged errand at mealtime because I may insult my palate with a drugstore sandwich, and, even worse, I may offend my stomach by leaving it empty. If there is reason to believe that a caller is hungry, even if it is someone whom he intends to take apart, he has Fritz bring a tray, and not scraps. As for interruptions at meals, for him there is absolutely nothing doing; when he is once in his chair at the table he leaves it only when the last bite of cheese or dessert is down. That's personal, but he has tried off and on to extend it to me, and he would if I would stand for it. The point is, does he hate to have my meal broken into because it interrupts his, or because it interrupts mine, or just on general principles? Search me.

Anyhow, he does. So when the phone rang while I was helping myself to another beef fillet, and Fritz answered it and came to say that Mrs. Vail wished to speak to Mr. Wolfe, and I pushed back my chair to go, Wolfe growled and glowered. He didn't tell me not to go, because he knew I would go anyway.

When I told our former client that Wolfe was at dinner and said he could call her back in half an hour, she said she wanted to see him. Now. I said okay, if she left in ten minutes he would be available when she arrived, and she said no, she couldn't come, she was worn out, and she sounded like it.

"That narrows it down," I told her, "if it's too private for the phone. Either I come there and get it and bring it back, or let it wait."

"It mustn't wait. Doesn't he *ever* go anywhere?"

"Not on business."

"Can you come now?"

I glanced at my wrist. "I can be there by nine o'clock. Will that do?"

She said she supposed it would have to, and I returned to the dining room and my place and asked Fritz to bring my coffee with my pie. The routine is back to the office for coffee because that's where the one and only chair is, and Wolfe's current book is there if I'm going out. When he had finished his pie and put his fork down, I said I was going to call on Mrs. Vail by request and asked for instructions.

He grunted. "Intelligence guided by experience. You know the situation. We owe her nothing."

I went. Having gone out to the stoop to feel the weather and decided I could survive without a coat, I walked to Eighth Avenue and got an uptown taxi. On the way uptown I looked it over. Wolfe's statement that I knew the situation left out something: I knew it from my angle, but not from his.. He might already have made some deduction, not final; for instance, that Noel Tedder was a kidnaper, a murderer, and a liar. Or sister Margot, or Uncle Ralph. It wouldn't be the first time, or even the twentieth, that he had kept a deduction to himself.

Noel must have been waiting in the hall, for two seconds after I pushed the button he opened the door. He did own some regular clothes—a plain dark gray suit, white shirt, and gray tie, but of course he might have bought them for the funeral. He shut the door, turned to

me, and demanded, "Why the hell did Wolfe tell Uncle
Ralph that Jimmy was murdered?"

"You may have three guesses," I told him. "Mine is
that he had to, since you had told Uncle Ralph that
someone had put something in Jimmy's drink and Mr.
Wolfe would explain it. Did you have to mention Jimmy's
drink?"

"No. That slipped out. But what the hell, if Wolfe's so
damn smart couldn't he have dodged it?"

"Sure he could. As for why he didn't, sometimes I
know why he does a thing while he's doing it, sometimes
I know an hour later, sometimes a week later, and sometimes never. Why, did Purcell tell your mother?"

"Certainly he did. There's hell to pay."

"All right, I'm the roving paymaster. Where is she?"

"What are you going to tell her?"

"I'll know when I hear myself. I play by ear. I told her
I'd be here by nine o'clock, and it's five after."

He thought he had more to say, decided he hadn't, told
me to come along, and led the way to the rear. I was
looking forward to seeing the library again, especially if
Benjamin Franklin was still there on the floor, but in the
elevator he pushed the button marked 3. When it stopped
I followed him out, along the hall, and into a room that
one glance told me would suit my wife fine if I ever had a
wife, which I probably wouldn't because she would probably want that kind of room. It was a big soft room—soft
lights, soft grays and pinks, soft rug, soft drapes. I
crossed the rug, after Noel, to where Mrs. Vail was flat in
a big bed, most of her covered by a soft pink sheet that
could have been silk, her head propped against a couple
of soft pink pillows.

"You may go, Noel," she said.

She looked terrible. Of course any woman is something
quite different if you see her without any make-up, but
even allowing for that she still looked terrible. Her face
was pasty, her cheeks sagged, and she was puffed up
around the eyes. When Noel had gone, closing the door,
she told me to sit down, and I moved a chair around.

"I don't know what good it will do, you coming," she
said. "I want to ask Nero Wolfe what he means by this

—this outrage. Telling my brother and my son that my husband was murdered. Can you tell me?"

I shook my head. "I can't tell you what he means by telling them. I assume you know why your son came to see him yesterday."

"Yes. To get him to help him find the money. When Noel asked me if he could have the money if he found it, I said yes. The money didn't matter; my husband was back. Now he's dead, and nothing matters. But he wasn't murdered."

So Noel had broached it. "Your son asked you again yesterday," I said, "and you said yes again. Didn't you?"

"I suppose I did. Nothing matters now, certainly that money doesn't— No, I'm wrong, something does matter. If you can't tell me why Nero Wolfe says my husband was murdered, then he will. If I have to go there, I will. I shouldn't, my doctor has ordered me to stay in bed, but I will."

I could see her tottering into the office supported by me, and Wolfe, after one look at her, getting up and marching out. He has done that more than once. "I can't tell you why Mr. Wolfe says it," I said, "but I can tell you why he thinks it." I might as well, since if I didn't Noel could. "Your husband was asleep on the couch when the rest of you left the room, leaving a light on. Right?"

"Yes."

"And the idea is that later he woke up, realized where he was, stood up, started for the door, lost his balance, grabbed at the statue, and pulled it down on him. Right?"

"Yes."

"That's what Mr. Wolfe won't take. He doesn't believe that a man awake enough to walk would be so befuddled that he couldn't dodge a falling statue. He realizes that he couldn't have been merely asleep when someone hauled him off the couch and over to the statue; he must have been unconscious. Since the autopsy found no sign that he had been slugged, he must have been doped. You had all been having drinks in the library, he had bourbon and water, so there had been opportunity to dope him. Therefore Mr. Wolfe deduces that he was murdered."

Her eyes were straight at me through the surrounding puffs. "That's absolutely ridiculous," she said.

I nodded. "Sure it is, to you. If Mr. Wolfe is right, then your daughter or your son or your brother or your lawyer, or you yourself, murdered Jimmy Vail. I think he's right, but I work for him. Granting that it wasn't you, you're up against a tough one. Naturally you would want whoever killed your husband to get what was coming to him, but naturally you wouldn't want your son or daughter or brother to get tagged for murder, and maybe not your lawyer. I admit that's tough, and I don't wonder that you say it's ridiculous. I wasn't trying to convince you of anything; I was just telling you why Mr. Wolfe thinks your husband was murdered. What else would you want to ask him if he was here?"

"I'd tell him he's a fool. A stupid fool."

"I'll deliver the message. What else?"

"I'd tell him that I have told my son that I'm taking back what I told him about the money, that he can have it if he finds it. He can't. I didn't know he would go to Nero Wolfe."

"You went to Nero Wolfe."

"That was different. I would have gone to the devil himself to get my husband back."

I gave my intelligence three seconds to be guided by experience before I spoke. "I'll deliver that message too," I said, "but I can tell you now what his reaction will be. He's stubborn and he's conceited, and he not only likes money, he needs it. Your son came to him and offered a deal, and he accepted it, and he won't let go just because you've changed your mind. If he can find that money he will, and he'll take his share. In my private opinion the chance of his finding it is about one in a million, but he won't stop trying. On the contrary. He's very sensitive. This attitude you're taking will make him try harder, and he might even do something peevish like writing a piece for a newspaper explaning why he has deduced that Jimmy Vail was murdered. That would be just like him. If you want some free advice, I suggest that you have your son in, here and now, and tell him you're *not* taking it back. I'll report it to Mr. Wolfe, and he'll decide if he wants to risk his time and money on a wild-goose chase."

It didn't work. As I spoke her lips kept getting tighter, and when I stopped she snapped, "He wouldn't get any share. Even if he found it. It's my money."

"That would be one for the lawyers. He would claim that his agreement with your son was based on an agreement your son had with you, made before witnesses. It would be the kind of mix-up lawyers love; they can juggle it around for years."

"You may go," she said.

"Sure." I rose. "But you understand—"

"Get out!"

I can take a hint. I walked out, shutting the door behind me, and proceeded to the elevator. When I emerged on the ground floor, there was Noel. He came to me.

"What did she say?" he squeaked.

"This and that." I caught a glimpse of someone through an arch. "She's a little upset. How about a little walk? If there's a bar handy, I could buy you a drink, provided it's not champagne."

He twisted his neck to glance up the stairs, brought his face back to me, said, "That's an idea," and went and opened the door. I passed through and onto the sidewalk, and he joined me. I suggested Barney's, at 78th and Madison, and we turned downtown.

A booth in a bar and grill is not an ideal spot for a private conversation. You can see if there is anyone in the booth in front of you curious enough to listen in, but you have to leave the one behind to luck or keep interrupting to look back. Noel and I got a break at Barney's. As we entered, a couple was leaving the booth at the far end, and we grabbed it, and I had a wall behind me. A white apron came and removed glasses and gave the table a swipe, and we ordered.

"So it's off," Noel said. "You couldn't budge her." I had told him en route how it stood.

"Not an inch." I was regretful, even gloomy. "You know why I wanted to buy you a drink? Because I wanted one myself. That talk with your mother took me back, back years ago, in Ohio. *My* mother. How old are you?"

"Twenty-three."

"I was only seventeen, just out of high school. But of

course the situation was different; it was easier for me than it would be for you. My mother wasn't wealthy like yours. I couldn't hit her for a hundred or a thousand or whatever I happened to need."

"Hell, neither can I. It's not that easy."

"It may not be easy, but the fact remains that she has it, and all you have to do is use the right approach. With me, with my mother, that wasn't the problem. She was a born female tyrant, and that was all there was to it. There wasn't a single goddam thing, big or little, that I could decide on my own. While your mother was talking I couldn't help thinking it was just too bad you couldn't do what I did."

The drinks came and we sampled them. Noel's sample was a gulp. "What did you do?" he asked.

"I told her to go to hell. One nice hot June day, the day after I graduated from high school, I told her to go to hell, and beat it. Of course I don't mean it literally, that it's too bad you can't do what I did. It's a different situation. You wouldn't have to. Now that Jimmy Vail's dead, you're the man of the house. All you'd have to do is just make it clear that you've got two feet of your own. Not in general terms like that, not just tell her to her face, 'Mother, I've got two feet of my own,' that wouldn't get you anywhere. It would have to be on a specific issue, and you couldn't ask for a better one than her taking back a definite promise she made you. That would be a beaut. You could tell her, 'Mother, you said I could have that money if I found it, and on the strength of that I made a deal with Nero Wolfe, and he'll hold me to it, and I'm going to hold you to it.' "

He took a swallow of gin and tonic. "She'd say it's her money."

"But it isn't. Not after what she told you before witnesses. She has given it to you, with only one condition attached, that you find it, and therefore it's a gift and you wouldn't have to pay tax on it. Granting that there's a slim chance of finding it, if we do find it you'll have four hundred thousand dollars in the till after you give Nero Wolfe his cut—no tax, no nothing. And even if we don't find it, you'll have let your mother know that you've got your own two feet, not by telling her so but by standing on them on a specific issue. There's another point, but we'll skip it."

"Why? What is it?"

I took a sip of scotch and soda. "It will be important only if Mr. Wolfe finds the money. If he does, one-fifth will be his, and don't think it won't. If your mother tries to keep him from getting it, or keeping it, the fur will fly, and some of it will be yours. If it gets to a court, you'll testify. For him."

"It wouldn't. It's not the money that's biting my mother, it's Jimmy. It's Wolfe's saying that Jimmy was murdered. Why the hell did he tell Uncle Ralph that?"

"He told you too."

"I had sense enough not to repeat it." He put his empty glass down. "Look, Goodwin, I don't give a damn. If Jimmy was murdered, someone that was there killed him, and I still don't give a damn. Of course it wasn't my mother, but even if it was, I'm not sure I'd give a damn even then. I'm supposed to be old enough to vote, but by God, the way I've had to knuckle under, you'd think I still wet the bed at night. You say I wouldn't have to do what you did, but if I had four hundred thousand dollars that's exactly what I'd do. I'd tell my mother to go to hell. I'm not as dumb as I look. I knew what I was doing Wednesday evening. I knew my mother was so glad her darling Jimmy was back she wouldn't stop to think, and I asked her about the money in front of witnesses, and I intended to go to Nero Wolfe the next morning, but the next morning Jimmy was dead, and that made it different. Now Wolfe has told Uncle Ralph Jimmy was murdered, I don't know why, and he has told my mother, and you tell me to show her I've got my own two feet. Balls. What if I haven't even got one foot?"

I signaled the white apron for refills. "Let's try something," I said and got out my notebook and pen and started writing. I dated a blank page at the top and wrote:

To Nero Wolfe: I hereby confirm the oral agreement we made yesterday. My mother, Mrs. Althea Vail, told me on Wednesday, April 26, and repeated on Friday, April 28, that if I find the $500,000 she gave a kidnaper on Tuesday, April 25, or any part of it, I may keep it for my own. Therefore that money belongs to me if I find it. I have engaged you to help me find it, and I have agreed that if you do find it, or any part of it, you are to keep one-fifth of the amount you find as payment for your services. I hereby confirm that agreement.

The refills had come, and I sampled mine as I read it over. Tearing the sheet out, I handed it to Noel and watched his face. He took his time, then looked up. "So what?"

"So you'd have a foot. I don't really expect you to sign it, I doubt if you have the nerve, you've knuckled under too long, but if you did sign it, you wouldn't have to tell your mother you were going to do so-and-so and stick to it. You could tell her you *had* done so-and-so, you had come here with me and talked it over and confirmed your agreement with Mr. Wolfe in writing. She couldn't send you to bed without any supper because you've already had your supper. Of course legally that thing isn't important, because you're already bound legally. Mr. Wolfe has a witness to his oral agreement with you. Me."

He started to read it over again, quit halfway, put his glass down, and extended his hand. "Give me that pen." I gave it to him, and he signed his name, pushed the paper across to me, picked up his glass, and raised it to eye level. "Excelsior! To freedom!" He put the glass to his mouth and drained it. A piece of ice slipped out and fell to the table, and he picked it up and threw it at the bartender across the room, missing by a yard. He shook his head, tittered, and asked me, "What did your mother do when you told her to go to hell?"

Since I had what I wanted, it would have suited me all right if we had been bounced, but apparently Noel was not a stranger at Barney's. The barkeep took no action beyond occasional glances in our direction to see if more ice was coming. Noel wanted to talk. The idea seemed to be that I had made a hero of him, and he wanted to know who or what had made a hero of me at the early age of seventeen. I was willing to spend another half-hour and another drink on him, but I suspected that he didn't want to go home until it was late enough for him to go to bed without stopping in his mother's room to say good night, and that might mean a couple of hours. So I began looking at my watch and worrying about being late for a date, and at ten o'clock I paid for the drinks and left him.

It was 10:26 when I mounted the stoop of the old brownstone and pushed the button. When Fritz opened the door he aimed a thumb to his rear, toward the office, signifying that there was company. I asked him who, and he told me in what he thinks is a whisper but is actually a kind of smothered croak, "Federal Bureau of Investigation." I told him, "Rub off all fingerprints and burn the papers," and went to the office.

You don't have to believe me, but I would have known after one look at him, even if Fritz hadn't told me. It's mostly the eyes and the jaw. An FBI man spends so much time pretending he's looking somewhere else that his eyes get confused; they're never quite sure it's okay to admit they're focused on you. His jaw is even worse off. It is given to understand that it belongs to a man who is intrepid, daring, dauntless, cool, long-headed, quick-witted, and hard as nails, but it is cautioned that he is also modest, polite, reserved, patient, bland, and never to be noticed in a crowd. No jaw on earth could handle that order. The only question is how often it will twitch, and sideways or up and down.

Wolfe said, "Mr. Goodwin. Mr. Draper."

Mr. Draper, having got to his feet, waited until my hand was unquestionably being offered, then extended his. Modest and reserved. His left hand went to a pocket, and I told him not to bother, but of course he did. An FBI man draws his credentials automatically, the way Paladin draws his gun. I glanced at it, not to hurt his feelings.

"Mr. Draper has been here a full hour," Wolfe said, with the accent on the 'full.' "He has a copy of the statement we signed, and he has asked many questions about details. He has covered the ground thoroughly, but he wanted to see you."

It looked like another full hour. I went to my desk and sat. Draper, back in the red leather chair, had his notebook out. "A few little questions, Mr. Goodwin," he said. "If you don't mind?"

"I like big ones better," I said, "but shoot."

"For the record," he said. "Of course you understand that; you're an experienced investigator. Mr. Wolfe says you left the house around half past six Tuesday evening, but he doesn't know when you returned. When did you?"

I permitted myself a grin, modest, polite, and bland. "Mr. Draper," I said, "I appreciate the compliment. You think I may have tailed Mrs. Vail Tuesday night, against her wishes and with or without Mr. Wolfe's consent, and that I may even have got as far as Iron Mine Road without being spotted by one of the kidnapers. As you know, that would have been one for the books, a real honey, and I thank you for the compliment."

"You're welcome. When did you return?"

I gave it to him complete, from six-thirty until one o'clock, places, names, and times, going slow enough for him to get it down. When I finished he closed the notebook, then opened it again. "You drive a car, don't you?"

"Mr. Wolfe owns it, I drive it. Sixty-one Heron sedan."

"Where is it garaged?"

"Curran, Tenth Avenue between Thirty-fifth and Thirty-sixth."

"Did you use the car Tuesday night?"

"No. I believe I mentioned taxis."

"Yes. You understand, Mr. Goodwin, for the record." He pocketed the notebook, arose, and got his hat from the stand. "You've been very helpful, Mr. Wolfe. Thank you very much. I doubt if we'll bother you again." He turned and went. I didn't get up, because an FBI man moves fast and I would have had to jump to get ahead of him to open the door. When I heard it close I went to the hall for a look, came back, got from my pocket the paper Noel had signed, and handed it to Wolfe.

He read it and put it down. "This was called for?"

"It seemed to be desirable. Would you like a report?"

"Yes."

I sat down and gave it to him—verbatim, all but the last half-hour with Noel, which wasn't material. When I was through he picked up the paper, read it again, nodded, and said, "Satisfactory." He put it down. "When your mother was in New York for a week last year, and dined here twice, and you spent some time taking her

around, I saw no trace of the animus you described to
Mr. Tedder."

"Neither did I. If we find enough of that five hundred
grand to make it worth telling about, and it gets printed
and she reads it, she won't mind. She understands that in
this job, working for you, the more lies the merrier, even
one about her. By the way, in a letter I got last week she
mentioned the chestnut croquettes again."

"Did you tell Fritz?"

"Sure. Anything for the morning?"

"No."

"Are Saul and Fred and Orrie still on?"

"Yes." He eyed me. "Archie. Your reply to Mr.
Draper's question. Could he have had any other reason
for asking it than the chronic suspicion of an inquisitor?"

"Certainly. They might have found the tire prints of
your car at Iron Mine Road. I drove it there Wednesday."

"Don't dodge. You have friends who would lie for you
without question, and you named some of them in your
reply. One particularly. How much of your reply was
fact?"

"All of it." I stood. "I'm going to bed. My ears are
burning. First the FBI and now you. I wish I *had* tailed
her, and Mr. Knapp with the suitcase; then we'd know
where the cabbage is."

11

It's always possible that people who invite me to the country
for a weekend will get a break; there's a chance that there
will be a development that will keep me in town, and they
will neither have to put me up nor put up with me. The
lucky ones that last weekend in April were a couple in
Easthampton who had me booked for Friday evening to
Monday morning. I have reported the developments of
Friday and Saturday, and Sunday I had to stick around in
case a call for reinforcements came from Saul or Fred or
Orrie.

Wolfe's routine for Sunday is different. Theodore
Horstmann, the orchid nurse, has the day off and goes to
visit his married sister in Jersey, so there are no regular

two-hour sessions in the plant rooms. Wolfe goes up once or twice to look around and do whatever chores the situation and the weather require, but there is no strict schedule. Usually he is down in the office by ten-thirty, at least the Sundays I am there, to settle down with the review-of-the-week section of the Sunday *Times*, which he goes right through.

From nine o'clock on that Sunday morning I was half expecting a call from Noel Tedder to tell me that he had issued his Declaration of Independence, one hero to another, but it hadn't come by the time I turned on the radio for the ten-o'clock news. Nor had there been any word from any of the tailers, but I was soon to know where Saul Panzer was. As I was turning the radio off the doorbell rang, and I went to the hall and saw Andrew Frost. So Saul was near enough to see the door opening, no matter how Frost had got there. I swung the door wide and said good morning.

It may be cheesy writing to say that Frost's expression and tone were frosty as he said he wanted to see Nero Wolfe, but it's good reporting. They were. It was possible that a factor was the probability that he would have to miss church, since he was dressed for it in a custom-made charcoal-gray top-coat and a forty-dollar homburg to match. I allowed him to enter, took the hat and coat, ushered him to the office, and buzzed the plant rooms on the house phone. When Wolfe's voice came, his usual testy "Yes?" and I told him Mr. Andrew Frost had come and had been admitted, he snapped, "Ten minutes," and hung up. When I told Frost he made a frosty little noise and gave me a frosty look. He didn't seem to look as much like Abraham Lincoln as he had Wednesday afternoon, but that may have been because I had never seen a picture of Lincoln simmering.

It was nearer fifteen minutes than ten when the sound came of the elevator, and Wolfe entered, a spray of Miltonia roezli in his left hand and the Sunday *Times* under his right arm. He takes his copy of the *Times* with him to the plant rooms so he won't have to stop off at his room on the way down to the office. Labor-saving device. He stopped at the corner of his desk to face the caller, said, "Mr. Frost? How do you do. I was expecting you," then put the flowers in the vase and the *Times* on the desk, and circled around to his chair.

Frost said distinctly, "You were not expecting me."

"But I was." Wolfe, seated, regarded him. "I invited you. I told Mr. Purcell that Mr. Vail was murdered, knowing that that would almost certainly bring you. I wished to see everyone who had been at that gathering Wednesday evening. You came, naturally, to remonstrate. Go ahead."

A muscle at the side of the lawyer's neck was twitching. "Are you saying," he demanded, "that you uttered that slander, knowing it was false, merely to coerce me to come here so you could see me?"

A corner of Wolfe's mouth went up a sixteenth of an inch. "That's quite a question. I uttered no slander, because what I said was true. I haven't coerced you; you are under no constraint; if you don't want to be here, go. Has Mr. Purcell told you what led me to the conclusion that Mr. Vail was murdered?"

"Yes. It's pure sophistry. The police and the District Attorney haven't formed that conclusion. It's false, fallacious, and defamatory, and it's actionable."

"Has the District Attorney made his final deduction and closed the inquiry?"

"Formally, no."

"Even if he does, that won't prove me wrong. He needs evidence that will convince a jury; I don't. I merely—"

"You'll need evidence if you persist in this slander and are made to answer for it."

"I doubt if I'll have to meet that contingency. I merely needed a starting point for a job I have undertaken, and I got it—my conclusion that Mr. Vail was murdered. I have no—"

"You have no job. You mean that fantastic scheme with Noel Tedder. That's off."

Wolfe turned his head. "Archie. That paper?"

I hadn't opened the safe, so I had to work the combination. I did so and got the paper from the shelf where I had put it before going up to bed. As I approached with it, Wolfe told me to give it to Frost. He took it, ran his eyes over it, and then read it word by word. When he looked up, Wolfe spoke.

"I'm not a counselor-at-law, Mr. Frost, but I have some knowledge of the validity of contracts. I'm confident that that paper binds Mrs. Vail as well as Mr. Tedder."

"When did he sign it?"

"Yesterday evening."

"It won't stand. He was tricked into signing it."

Wolfe turned. "Archie?"

"No tricks," I told Frost. "Ask him. He's fed up and wants to stand on his own two feet. I bought him three little drinks, but he was perfectly sober. There were witnesses."

"Witnesses where?"

"Barney's bar and grill, Seventy-eighth and Madison." I was still there by him, and I put out a hand. "May I have it, please?"

He took another look at it and handed it over. I went to the safe and put it back on the shelf and swung the door shut.

Wolfe was speaking. "I was about to say, Mr. Frost, that I have no intention of broadcasting my conclusion that Mr. Vail was murdered, or my reasons for it. I had to tell Mr. Tedder in order to explain my approach to our joint problem, and I told Mr. Purcell because I wanted to see you; he would of course tell his sister, and she would tell you. My purposes have been served. As for the murder, I am not—"

"There was no murder."

"That's *your* conclusion—or your delusion. I'm not bent on disturbing it. I am not a nemesis."

"Why did you want to see me?"

"When I know that one of a group of people has committed a murder, and possibly two murders, and I need to know which one, I like to look at them and hear them—"

"Then you *are* persisting in the slander. You're saying that you intend to identify one of the people there Wednesday evening as a murderer."

"Only to my satisfaction, for my private purpose. Perhaps my explanation has lost something on its way to you through Mr. Purcell and Mrs. Vail. No. I'm wrong. I explained fully to Mr. Tedder, but not to Mr. Purcell. Hav-

ing deduced that Mr. Vail was murdered, I made two assumptions: that the murder was consequent to the kidnaping and therefore the murderer had been involved in
the kidnaping, and that he or she knows who has the
money and where it is or might be. So I needed to identify him and I had to see all of you. I had seen Mrs. Vail.
I intend to find that money."

Frost was shaking his head, his lips compressed. "It's
hard to believe. I know your reputation, but this is incredible. You wanted to see me so that, by looking at me
and hearing me, you could decide if I was a kidnaper and
a murderer? Preposterous!"

"It does seem a little overweening," Wolfe conceded,
"but I didn't rely solely on my acumen." He turned. "Archie, bring Saul."

That shows you his opinion of Saul. Not "Archie, see if
Saul is around." Frost was Saul's subject, so, since Frost
was here, Saul was in the neighborhood. Of course it was
my opinion too. I went to the front door and out to the
stoop, descended two steps, stood, and beckoned to Manhattan, that part of it north of 35th Street. A passer-by
turned his head to see who I was inviting, saw no one,
and went on. I was expecting Saul to appear from behind
one of the parked cars across the street, and I didn't see
him until he was out of an area-way and on the sidewalk,
on this side, thirty paces toward Tenth Avenue. He had
figured that Frost would head west to get an uptown taxi,
and undoubtedly he would. Reaching me, he asked, "Was
I spotted?"

"You know damn well you weren't spotted. You're
wanted. We need you for four-handed pinochle."

He came on up, and we entered and went to the office,
Saul in front. Sticking his cap in his pocket, he crossed to
Wolfe's desk with no glance at Frost and said, "Yes, sir?"

Wolfe turned to Frost. "This is Mr. Saul Panzer. He
has been making inquiries about you since yesterday
morning." Back to Saul: "Have you anything to add to
your report on the phone last evening?"

Presumably after I had left to go to Mrs. Vail. Saul
said, "Only one item, from a source I saw after I phoned.
Last fall he bought a one-third interest in a new twelve-

story apartment house on Eighty-third Street and Park Avenue."

"Briefly, some of the items you reported yesterday."

"He's a senior member of the firm of McDowell, Frost, Hovey, and Ulrich, One-twenty Broadway. Twenty-two names on the letterhead. He was co-chairman of the Committee of New York Lawyers for Nixon. Two years ago he gave his son a house in East Sixty-eighth Street for a wedding present. He's a director in at least twenty corporations—I don't think the list I got is complete. He was Harold F. Tedder's counsel for more than ten years. He has a house on Long Island, near Great Neck, thirty rooms and eleven acres. In nineteen fifty-four President Eisenhower—"

"That's enough." Wolfe turned. "As you see, Mr. Frost, I realize that my perspicacity is not infallible. Of course some of Mr. Panzer's items invite further inquiry —for example, is the estate on Long Island unencumbered? Is there a mortgage?"

Frost was no longer frosty; he was too near boiling. "This is unbelievable," he declared. He was close to sputtering. "You have actually paid this man to collect a dossier on me? To examine the possibility that I'm a kidnaper and murderer? Me?"

Wolfe nodded. "Certainly. You're a lawyer with wide experience; you know I could exclude no one who was there. Mr. Panzer is discreet and extremely competent; I'm sure he—"

The doorbell rang. I got up and went to the hall for a look, returned to my desk, scribbled "Cramer" on the scratch pad, tore off the sheet, and handed it to Wolfe. He glanced at it, closed his eyes, opened them in three seconds, and turned to Frost.

"Inspector Cramer of the police is at the door. If you would prefer not to—"

Frost's wires snapped. He jerked forward, his eyes blazing. "Damn you! *Damn* you! You phoned him!"

"I did not," Wolfe snapped. "He is uninvited and unexpected. I don't know why he's here. He deals only with death by violence. If he has heard of my conclusion that Mr. Vail was murdered, I don't know when or from

whom. Not from Mr. Goodwin or me." The doorbell
rang. "Do you want him to know you are here?"

"You're a liar! You're to blame—"

"Enough!" Wolfe hit the desk. "The situation is precisely as I have described it. Archie, admit Mr. Cramer.
Do you want him to see you or not? Yes or no."

"No," Frost said, and left the chair. Wolfe told Saul to
take him to the front room, and when Saul had gone to
the connecting door and opened it, and Frost was moving, I went to admit the law. From the expression on Cramer's face I expected him to march on by to the office,
but when I turned after shutting the door, he was there
facing me.

"What were you doing with Noel Tedder last night?"
he demanded.

"Don't snap my head off," I said. "I'd rather tell you
before a witness. Mr. Wolfe will do." I walked to the office, entered, and told Wolfe, "He wants to know what I
was doing with Noel Tedder last night. He didn't say
please."

Cramer was at my elbow. "The day I say please to
you," he growled, and went to the red leather chair, sat,
and put his hat on the stand.

"I suppose," Wolfe said, "it's futile to complain. You
have been a policeman so long, and have asked so many
people so many impertinent questions, and so frequently
have got answers to them, that it has become sponta-
neous. Have you any ground at all for expecting Mr.
Goodwin to answer that one?"

"We might arrange a deal," I suggested. "I'll ask an
impertinent question. Why have you got a tail on Noel
Tedder if Jimmy Vail's death was an accident?"

"We haven't got a tail on him."

"Then how did you know he was with me?"

"A detective happened to see you with him on the
street and followed you." Cramer turned to Wolfe. "Day
before yesterday you refused to tell me where you and
Goodwin had been for twenty-four hours. You said you
had no further commitment to Mrs. Vail and you had no
client. You repeated that in your signed statement. You
did not repeat it to Draper of the FBI when he asked you
last night. Your answer was evasive. That's not like you.

I have never known you to hedge on a lie. Now this, Goodwin with Noel Tedder. You're not going to tell me that was just social. Are you?"

"No."

"Goodwin?"

"No."

"Then what was it?"

Wolfe shook his head. "You have a right to expect answers only to questions that are relevant to a crime. What crime are you investigating?"

"That's typical. That's you. I'm investigating the possibility that Jimmy Vail didn't die by accident."

"Then you aren't satisfied that he did."

"Satisfied, no. The District Attorney may be, I don't know, you can ask him. I say I have a right to expect Goodwin to answer that question. Or you."

Wolfe tilted his chair back, then his head, pursed his lips, and examined the ceiling. Cramer took a cigar from a pocket, rolled it between his palms, which was silly with a cigar that wasn't going to be lit, held it at an angle with his thumb and forefinger, frowning at it, and returned it to his pocket. Evidently he had asked it an impertinent question and it has refused to answer. Wolfe let his chair come forward and said, "The paper, Archie." I went to the safe and got it from the shelf and took it to him. He put it on his desk pad and turned to Cramer.

"I think you have the notion that I have withheld information from you on various occasions just to be contrary. I haven't. I have reserved details only when I wanted them, at least temporarily, for my exclusive use, or when you have been excessively offensive. Today you have been reasonably civil, though of course not affable; imparting it will not make it less useful to me; and if it furthers your investigation, though I confess I don't see how it can, it will serve a double purpose." He picked up the paper. "I'll read it. I won't hand it to you because you would probably say it may be needed as evidence, which would be absurd, and pocket it."

He read it, ending, "Signed by Noel Tedder. It isn't holograph; Mr. Goodwin wrote it. I answered that question by Mr. Draper ambiguously because if I had told him of my agreement with Mr. Tedder he would have kept me up all night, thinking that I had some knowledge, at least an inkling, of where the money might be found. I have no commitment to Mrs. Vail, but I do have a client: Noel Tedder."

"Yeah." It came out hoarse, and Cramer cleared his throat. He always gets a little hoarse when he talks with Wolfe, probably a certain word or words sticking in his throat. "And either you have some idea where the money is or this is a cover for something else. Does Mrs. Vail know about that agreement?"

"Yes."

"And that's what Goodwin and Tedder were discussing last night?"

"Yes."

"What else were they discussing?"

Wolfe turned. "Archie?"

I shook my head. "Nothing. We touched on mothers some, his and mine, but that was in connection with the agreement."

"So your question is answered," Wolfe told him. "I'm aware that you'll pass it on to Mr. Draper, but he isn't here, and if he comes he won't get in. We have given him all the information we possess about the kidnaping, with no reservations. I do have an idea where the money is, but it is based—"

"By God, you admit it."

"I state it. It's based on deductions and assumptions I have made, not on any evidence I'm withholding. That applies not only to the kidnaping and the whereabouts of the money, but also to the death of Mr. Vail. What would you say if I told you that I'm convinced that he was murdered, with premeditation, and that I think I know, I'm all but certain that I know, who killed him and why?"

"I'd say you were grandstanding. It wouldn't be the first time. I know you. God, do I know you! When you've really got something you don't say you're convinced and you're all but certain. You say you *know*. If you've got any evidence that he was murdered and that points to the murderer, I want it, and I want it now. Have you got any?"

"No."

"Then I'll leave you to your deductions and assump-

tions." He picked up his hat. "You're damn right I'll tell
Draper." He rose. "But if he knew you as well as I do—
Oh, nuts." He turned and marched out.

I stepped to the hall and saw him close the front door
behind him, stepped back in, and asked Wolfe, "So
you're all but certain? Do you know what 'grandstanding'
means. Where did you get the idea—"

"Get Saul."

He snapped it. I went and opened the door to the front
room and told Saul to come. As he entered, Wolfe spoke.
"Mr. Frost has gone?"

Saul nodded. "He bent his ear for five minutes trying
to hear you, found that he couldn't on account of the
sound-proofing, and left."

"I want Fred. If Mr. Purcell is at home, he will of
course be nearby. Bring him as soon as possible." His
eyes came to me. "Archie, I want Mr. Tedder, and Orrie
with him. Also as soon as possible. Don't stop to tell
Fritz about the door. I'll see that it's bolted."

"You want me back," Saul said.

"Yes. Go."

We went.

12

It wouldn't do, of course, for me to ring the Vail house
and get Noel and tell him Wolfe wanted to see him. One,
he might not come without some fancy persuading. Two,
Wolfe wanted Orrie too, and Orrie, tailing him, might
possibly lose him on the way downtown. Three, Saul had
to go there to get Fred, and the taxi fare is the same for
two as for one. So we walked to Tenth Avenue and
flagged a cab.

It was 11:23 of a sunny Sunday morning, nice and
warm for the last of April, when we stopped at the curb
in front of 994 Fifth Avenue, paid the hackie, and got
out. When we're going on with the program, the method
of getting in touch with a tail, understood by all of us, is
a little complicated, but in that case it was simple. We
merely raised an arm to wave at a squirrel in a tree in the
park and started to stroll downtown. Before we had taken

twenty steps Fred appeared from behind a parked car across the street and came over to us and said if we had come an hour sooner he could have gone to church.

"It would take more than church to square you," I told him. "Purcell hasn't shown?"

"No."

"What about Orrie?"

"His subject showed at ten fifty-one and led him away." Fred looked at Saul. "And yours came at eleven-fifteen in a cab and went in. So you got shook for once?"

"No," I said, "he got called off. Did Tedder ride or walk?"

"Walked. Turned east at Seventy-eighth Street. Orrie was keeping distance. Something happened? What's up?"

"God doesn't know but Mr. Wolfe does. Everybody in for a conference." I turned to Saul. "If you and Fred go on down, you can read the Bible until I bring Tedder and Orrie. There are five versions in four different languages on the second shelf from the top near the left end. I'm thinking where to start looking for him. I think better when I talk."

"We can't help you think," Saul said, "because you know him and we don't, but we can help you look. Of course, if he wanted a taxi, it's Sunday and he could have got one here on Fifth, or if he thought he'd get one quicker on Madison he wouldn't have gone to Seventy-eighth to turn east. But if he has a car and it's garaged on Seventy-eighth, he—"

"No," Fred said. "Four cars garaged on Eighty-second Street. I've seen three of them." As I said, Fred was a little too solid for quick reactions, but give him time and he would collect a lot of miscellaneous information that might be useful.

"Okay," I said, "thanks a lot for doing my thinking. Now I know where he is, maybe. If you've thought wrong and he's not there, we might as well go back to Thirty-fifth Street and sing hymns until Orrie phones. Come along."

It was one chance in a thousand, but it was the only chance there was. I led them south to Seventy-eighth Street and east to Madison Avenue, halted in front of Barney's, and told them, "We might as well give Orrie the high sign first and have him join us. Then when I bring—"

"There he is," Saul said.

I turned. Orrie had emerged from a doorway across the street and was crossing the sidewalk. "All I need," I said, "is someone to do my thinking," and stepped to Barney's door and entered.

There was no one at the bar, since it was Sunday morning, and there weren't many at the tables or in the booths, but the top of a head was showing in the booth at the far end and I went to it. It was Noel, with a plate of roast turkey and trimmings in front of him, untouched, and a nearly empty glass in his hand. He looked up at me, blinked, and squeaked, "Well, for God's sake!"

I gave him a friendly grin, hero to hero. "This isn't luck," I said, "it's fate. When I learned you had gone out, it wasn't that I had a hunch, I just started to walk, and there I was in front of Barney's, and I came in, and here you are. Have you—uh—spoken to your mother?"

"No." He emptied the glass and put it down. "I was going to go up to her room right after breakfast, but then I thought I'd better wait. I thought I'd better kind of work up to it. I wanted to go over everything you said. So I came here to this booth where you said it. Sit down and oil your throat."

"Thanks, but I'm on an errand. You won't have to tell your mother you're big enough to shave; she knows it. Andrew Frost came to see Mr. Wolfe this morning, and Mr. Wolfe showed him the paper you signed, and Frost went to see your mother. He's there now."

"The hell he is. Holy Christ."

"And Mr. Wolfe sent me to bring you. I think he has an idea where the money is, but if so he didn't tell me; he wants to tell you. He said as soon as possible, which means now. You haven't touched your turkey."

"To hell with the turkey. Frost is with my mother?"

"Right."

"And Wolfe wants to see me?"

"Right."

"He slid out of the booth and got erect. "Look. You see me?"

"I do."

"Am I standing on my own two feet?"

"You are."

"Check. Let's go."

The waiter was approaching, and as Noel didn't seem to see him, I asked him how much. He said four-twenty, and I gave him a finiff and followed Noel to the door.

Outside, Saul had performed as usual. There were two taxis at the curb. The one in front was empty, and the trio were in the one in the rear. He had even arranged for a signal so the hackie wouldn't take the wrong passengers; as Noel and I crossed the sidewalk the horn of the cab in the rear let out a grunt.

When we stopped in front of the old brownstone at ten minutes past noon, and I paid the hackie and climbed out after Noel, the other taxi wasn't in sight. Saul again. He didn't know whether Wolfe wanted Noel to know that the whole army was mobilized, so he was hanging back to give us time to get inside. I had to ring, since the bolt was on. Fritz let us in, and I took Noel to the office. It had been just sixty-five minutes since Wolfe had told Saul and me to fetch. If I may say so, I would call that as soon as possible.

Wolfe did something remarkable: he left his chair and took two steps to offer Noel a hand. Either he was telling me that Noel was not a murderer, or he was telling Noel that he was with friends and since he could count on us we would expect to count on him. Of course Noel didn't appreciate it; a man who will some day be in the top bracket without trying has plenty of hands offered to him. He took the red leather chair and said, "Goodwin says you know where the money is."

"Correction," I objected. "I said I think he has an idea where it is."

Wolfe grunted. He eyed Noel. "The truth is somewhere between. I'm fairly certain. Call it a presumption. To test it we need your cooperation, your active assistance. Even with it, it may be difficult—"

The doorbell rang. I told Wolfe, "Three of my friends," and stood. "I'll put them in the front room."

"No," he said, "bring them."

So it was to be a family party. I went and let them in, told them they could come and sit with the quality if they would behave themselves, and followed them to the office. Wolfe greeted them and turned to the client. "Mr. Tedder, shake hands with Mr. Panzer. Mr. Durkin. Mr. Cather."

The very best corn. I had seldom seen him sink so low. I moved chairs up, and they sat. Wolfe's eyes took them in, left to right, then back to focus on Noel. "Time may be of vital importance, so I won't waste it. The money, all of it, half a million dollars in cash, is at your house in the country. If not in the house, it's on the premises."

"Jesus," Noel said.

"It would take all afternoon to explain fully all the circumstances that have led me to that conclusion, and I don't want to take even half an hour. You think I have sagacity, or you wouldn't have come to me with your problem. You'll accept that—"

"Wait a minute. How did the money get there?"

"Mr. Vail took it there. He took the suitcase from your mother at Iron Mine Road. You'll accept—"

"But my God, why did he—"

"Mr. Tedder. You could ask a thousand questions; I said it would take all afternoon. Do you want that money?"

"You're damn right I want it."

"Then take my conclusion on my word, tentatively at least. I say the money is there. Who is at that house now?"

"No one. Only the caretaker."

"No other servants?"

"No. We don't use it before the middle of May. Usually later."

"This is Sunday. Not on weekends?"

"We did when my father was alive, but not now. My mother says it's too cold until June."

"Mr. Vail went there last weekend. Saturday morning. What for?"

"To see about the roof and some other things. The caretaker said the roof was leaking."

"What's the caretaker's name?"

"Waller. Jake Waller."

"Are you on amicable terms with him?"

"Why, I guess so. Sure."

"A leaky roof should be attended to. How likely is it that your mother or sister or uncle will go there today to see to it?"

"My mother certainly won't. It's possible that my sister or my uncle will, but they haven't said anything about it so far as I know."

"Is the house locked up?"

"I suppose the doors are locked, yes."

"Have you a key?"

"Not now I haven't. I have one in the summer."

"Would the caretaker let you in?"

"Certainly he would. Why wouldn't he?"

Wolfe turned. "Archie. Will anyone be guarding that place? County or state or federal?"

I shook my head. "What for? Not unless someone has got to the same conclusion as you, which I doubt."

Back to Noel. "Mr. Tedder. I suggest that if you want that money you go there and get it. Now. Mr. Goodwin will drive my car. Mr. Panzer, Mr. Durkin, and Mr. Cather will go with you. They are competent, reliable, and experienced. My chef has prepared a hamper of food which you can eat on the way; it will be acceptable to your palate and your stomach. I have no suggestions as to your procedure when you get there; I didn't know Mr. Vail; you did. He returned to that house Wednesday morning with the suitcase in his car, and his time was rather limited. He wanted to act naturally, and naturally he would want to come to New York, where his wife was, without undue delay. According to the caretaker, in the published reports, he arrived about half past seven, and he left for New York around nine o'clock. Meanwhile he had bathed, shaved, changed his clothes, and eaten, so he hadn't spent much time on disposal of the suitcase; but it is highly likely that he had known on Saturday that he would bring it there for concealment and he had probably made preparations. You knew him and you must have some notion of how his mind worked, so ask yourself: where on those premises would he hide the suitcase? He anticipated no intensive search for it, since he thought it would never be suspected that he had got it and brought it there; what he had to make sure of was that it would not be accidentally discovered by a member of the family or a servant. I presume you know what the suitcase looked like?"

"Sure. Who doesn't?"

Wolfe nodded. "From the published descriptions. I think you may safely expect to find *that* suitcase. There was no reason for him to transfer the money to another container, and there was good reason not to; he would have had the added problem of disposing of the suitcase." Wolfe's head turned to take us in. "There it is, gentlemen, unless you have questions. If you have, let them be to the point. I wish you luck."

Noel squeaked, "I hope to God . . ." He let it hang.

"Yes, Mr. Tedder?"

"Nothing." Noel stood up. "Hell, what can I lose that I've got? Let's go."

I went to the kitchen to get the hamper.

13

About two miles northeast of Katonah you turn off the highway, right, pass between two stone pillars, proceed up the graveled drive, an easy slope, winding, about four hundred yards, and there is the house, old gray stone with high steep roofs. At a guess, not as many rooms as Frost's on Long Island—say twenty-five, maybe less. Trees and other things with leaves, big and little, were all around, and a lot of lawn, but although I can't qualify as an expert I had the impression that they weren't getting quite enough attention. Saul eased the Heron to a stop a foot short of the bushes that bordered a surfaced rectangle at the side of the house, and we climbed out. He was at the wheel because at Hawthorne Circle I had decided that I could use some of the contents of the hamper, which they had all been working on, and I don't like one-handed driving.

Noel, in between bites of sturgeon or cheese or rhubarb tart, or swallows of wine, had briefed us on the prospect and answered questions. The house itself looked like the best bet. Not only was there no likely spot in the stable, which no longer held horses, or the kennels, which no longer held dogs, but also Jimmy would have risked being seen by the caretaker if he had lugged a suitcase to one of them in the open. Nor was there any likely spot in the garage, which was connected with the house. The only other outbuilding was a six-room stone structure in the rear, living quarters for servants, occupied now only by the caretaker. Something really fancy, like wrapping the suitcase in plastic and burying it somewhere on the grounds, was of course out, with the caretaker around. The house was the best bet, and not the cellar, since there was no part of it that the caretaker might not poke around in, or, later, if the suitcase was to stay put for a while, a servant or even a member of the family.

As we climbed out a man appeared from around a corner—a tall, lanky specimen in a red wool shirt and dungarees who hadn't shaved for at least three days. As he caught sight of Noel he spoke. "Oh, it's you, Mr. Tedder?"

"On my own two feet," Noel said, meeting him and offering a hand. Either he believed in democracy or Wolfe had made it a habit. "How are you, Jake?"

"I'll make out if they don't trip me." Jake gave us a glance. "The roof, huh? We had a shower Friday and it leaked again. I phoned your mother."

"She's been . . . not so good."

Jake nodded. "Too bad about Mr. Vail. Terrible thing. You know they've been after me, but what could I tell 'em? For nearly a week all kinds of people drivin' in. I'm takin' no chances." His hand went to his hip pocket and came out with a gun, an old black Marley .32. He patted it. "Maybe I couldn't hit a rabbit, but I can scare 'em off." He put it back. "You want to see in your mother's room where it leaked?"

"Not today, Jake." Noel's squeak wasn't so squeaky; perhaps his voice was changing. "My mother may be out this week. These men are detectives from New York and they want to look around in the house. They think there may be something—I don't know exactly what. You know how detectives are. Is there a door open?"

Jake nodded. "The back door's open, the one off the kitchen. I cook and eat in the kitchen, better tools there. Your mother knows I do. Lucky I had bacon and eggs on hand when he came Wednesday morning. Terrible thing

about him. I sure do know how detectives are, I do now."
He looked at us. "No offense to you fellows."

Obviously one of us ought to say something, so I said,
"We don't offend easy. We know how caretakers are
too."

"I bet you do." He chuckled. "I just bet you do. You
want me to help with anything, Mr. Tedder?"

"No, thanks. We'll make out. This way, Goodwin."
Noel headed for the corner Jake had come from, and we
followed.

To prove how competent and experienced we are I
could describe the next forty minutes in detail, but it
wouldn't help you any more than it did us. We had
learned from Noel that the possibilities were limited.
Jimmy Vail had been a town man and had never got inti-
mate with this country place. His bedroom was the only
spot in the house he had had personal relations with, so
we tried that first, but after we had looked in the two clo-
sets and the bottom drawer of a chest, then what? The
bed was a big old walnut thing with a canopy, and there
was enough room under it for an assortment of wardrobe
trunks, but room was all there was.

We went all around, downstairs and up. We even spent
ten minutes in the cellar, most of it in a storage room
where there were some ancient pieces of luggage along
with the other stuff. We looked in the garage, which was
big enough for five cars, and there in a corner saw something that would have seemed promising if it hadn't been
there in the open where anyone might have lifted the lid
—a big old-fashioned trunk. I did lift the lid and saw
something that took me back to my boyhood days in
Ohio. But a couple of cardboard boxes had held my two-
year collection of birds' eggs, and here were dozens of
compartments, some with one egg and some with two or
three. I asked Noel if they were his, and he said no, they
had been his father's, and the trunk held more than three
hundred different kinds of eggs. I lifted the tray out, and
underneath it was another tray, not so many compartments but bigger eggs. Orrie came for a look and said,
"Let's take that. It may not be worth half a million, but
it's worth something." I put the top tray back in and was
shutting the lid when I heard the sound of a car.

The garage doors were closed and the sound was faint, but I have good ears. The parking area where we had left the Heron was on this side of the house, but not in front of the garage. The door we had come through was standing open—the door from the garage to a back hall. I stepped to it quietly and poked my head through, and in a moment heard a voice I had heard before. Margot Tedder. She was asking Jake whose car that was. Then Jake, telling her: her brother Noel and four detectives from New York who were searching the house for something. Margot asked, searching for what? Jake didn't know. Then Margot calling her brother, a healthier yell than I thought she had in her: "Noel! *Noel!!*"

Preferring the garage to the outdoors as a place for a conference, I sang out, "We're in the garage!" and turned and told Noel, "It's your sister."

"I know it is. Damn her."

"I'll do the talking. Okay?"

"Like hell you will. She'll do the talking."

It's a pleasure to work with men who can tell time. Saul had started to move when I called out that we were in the garage, and Fred and Orrie a second later, and I had moved back from the door, taking Noel with me. So when Margot appeared and headed for Noel, with Jake right behind her, and Uncle Ralph behind Jake, all my three colleagues had to do was take another step or two and they were between the newcomers and the exit. And both Saul and Orrie were only arm's length from Jake's hip pocket. It's a real pleasure.

I was at Noel's side. As Margot approached she gave me a withering glance, then switched it to Noel, stopped in front of him, and said, "You utter idiot. Get out and take your gang with you."

I said politely, "It's as much his house as yours, Miss Tedder, and he got here first. What if he tells you to get out?"

She didn't hear me. "You heard me, Noel," she said. "Take this scum and go."

"Go yourself," Noel said. "Go to hell."

She about-faced and started for the door. I raised my voice a little. "Block it! Saul, you'd better get it."

"I have it," Saul said and raised his hand to show me

the gun he had lifted from Jake's pocket. Margot saw it
and stopped. Fred and Orrie had filled the doorway.
Uncle Ralph made a noise. Jake looked at Margot, then
at Noel, and back at Margot. Saul was back of him, and
he didn't know he had been disarmed.

"You wouldn't shoot," Margot said scornfully, and I
have to admit there was no shake in her voice.

"No," I told her back, "he wouldn't shoot, but why
should he? Five against three, granting that you're one
and Jake is with you. As Jake told you, we're looking for
something, and we haven't finished. Noel told you to go,
but it would be better for you to stay here in the garage,
all three of you, until we're through. One of you might
use the phone, and we'd be interrupted. I don't—"

I stopped because she was moving. She went to the
door, just short of Fred and Orrie, just not touching
them, and said, "Get out of the way."

Orrie smiled at her. He thinks he knows how to smile
at girls, and as a matter of fact he does. "We'd like to,"
he said, "but we're glued."

"I don't know how long we'll be," I told her, "but
there's a stack of chairs there by the wall. Fred and Orrie,
you—"

"Jake! Go and phone my mother!" Her voice still
didn't shake, but it was a little shrill.

And by gum, Jake's hand went back to his hip pocket.
I was almost sorry his gun was gone; it would have been
interesting to see how he handled it. His jaw dropped,
and he wheeled and saw it in Saul's hand. "It's all right,"
Saul said, "you'll get it back." Jake turned to Noel and
said, "Fine lot you brought." He turned to Margot. "I
guess I can't."

"You guess right," I told him. "Fred and Orrie, you
stay here and keep the peace. Noel and Saul and I will
look around some more. But it has occurred to me that I
may have overlooked something. Wait till I see." I went
to the corner where the big trunk was, lifted the lid, took
out the top tray, and put it on the floor gently. Then I
reached in and got the loops at the ends of the second
tray and eased it up and out, and I damn near dropped it.
There at the bottom of the trunk was an old tan leather
suitcase. I took three seconds out to handle my controls,

staring at it, then carefully put the tray on the floor to one side, straightened up, and said, "Come and take a look, Noel." He came and stooped over to see, then reached a hand in and heaved, and out it came. At that point I decided that he might really have two feet. I had expected him to squeak something like "Jesus Holy Christ what the hell," but he squeaked nothing. He just reached in and got it, put it on the floor, undid the clasps, and opened the lid; and there was the biggest conglomeration of engraved lettuce I had ever had the pleasure of looking at. I glanced around. Purcell was at my elbow, and Jake was at his elbow, and Saul was right behind them. Margot was approaching, hips stiff as ever. Noel, squatting, with a hand flattened out on top of the find, tilted his head back to look up at me and said, "I didn't believe him, but I thought I might as well come. How in the name of God did he know it was here?"

Orrie, still in the doorway with Fred, called over, "Damn it, have you got it?" Margot was saying something which I didn't bother to hear, and Purcell was making noises. I looked at my wrist; it's nice to know exactly what time you found half a million bucks. Eight minutes to three. I went and put the trays back in the trunk, gently and carefully, closed the lid and came back. Noel was fastening the lid of the suitcase, paying no attention to what his sister was saying.

"Okay," I said, "we'll move. Saul and Noel will take it out to the car." I put out a hand to Saul. "The gun. I'll unload it and leave it on the kitchen table. Fred and Orrie will follow Saul and Noel. I'll stay in the kitchen to guard the phone until you have the car turned around and headed out. When you tap the horn I'll come. Miss Tedder, if you came to see about the leaky roof, don't neglect it just because we got in the way. As Mr. Wolfe remarked to your brother just this afternoon, a leaky roof should be attended to."

14

When the doorbell rang at five minutes to six Monday afternoon I was in my chair in the office, leaning back, my feet up on the corner of the desk, looking at the headline on the front page of the *Gazette*:

VAIL RANSOM FOUND
$500,000 in Birds' Egg Trunk

With that second hot exclusive given to Lon Cohen in three days, our credit balance with him was colossal. The picture of the suitcase on page 3, with the lid open, had been taken by me. The article, which I had read twice, was okay. I was given a good play, and so was Wolfe, and Saul and Fred and Orrie were named. I had given Lon nothing about Margot or Uncle Ralph, but had mentioned Jake's gun. A gun improves any story.

The money was in the bank, but not the one it had come from. Noel had demonstrated that he was neither piker nor a soft touch. When I had put the suitcase on the couch in the office, and he had opened it, and we had all gathered around to admire the contents, including Wolfe, he had taken out a couple of bundles of cees, counted off two grand and handed it to Orrie, then two grand to Fred, two to Saul, and five to me. Then he had asked Wolfe, "Do you want yours now?" and Wolfe had said it would have to be counted first since his share was a percentage; and Wolfe had gone to the kitchen to tell Fritz there would be four guests for dinner. It was then five o'clock, but at seven, just two hours later, Fritz had served us the kind of meal you read about. No shad roe.

The arrangement for the night was determined by two facts: one, there wasn't room in the safe; and two, Noel didn't want to take it home, which was understandable. So when bedtime came I got pajamas for him and took him up to the south room, which is above Wolfe's, checked the towel supply and turned the bed down, and took the suitcase up another flight to my room. It wouldn't go under my pillow, so I made room for it on the bed stand right against the pillow. We hadn't counted the money.

It was counted Monday morning in a little room at the Continental Bank and Trust Company on Lexington Avenue, where Wolfe has had his account for twenty years. Present were an assistant vice-president, two tellers, and Noel and me. Of course Noel and I were merely spectators. They started on it a little after ten, and it was a quarter past twelve when they declared finally and positively that the figure was $489,000. Noel took twenty twenties for pocket money; $100,000 was deposited in Wolfe's account; and an account was opened for Noel with a balance of $388,600. There would be no service charge, the assistant vice-president told Noel, with a banker's smile at his own hearty joke. We had said nothing about where it had come from, and he had asked no questions, since Wolfe was an old and valued customer, but he must have had a guess if he ever looked at a newspaper. Of course the *Gazette* wasn't out yet.

Noel and I shook hands in parting, out on the sidewalk. He took a taxi headed uptown. I didn't hear what he said to the hackie, but I gave myself five to one that he was going straight to 994 Fifth Avenue. A nice little bank balance in his own name is very good for a man's feet. I took a little walk to call on Lon Cohen.

I rather expected some kind of communication from Mrs. Vail or Andrew Frost before the day was out, but the afternoon went by without a peep. I also rather expected that Wolfe would put on a strutting act, his own special brand of strutting, explaining how simple it had been to dope out where the money was, but he didn't, and I wasn't going to pamper him by asking for it. I got back in time to dispose of the morning mail, which was skimpy, before lunch, and after lunch he finished his book and got another one from the shelf, and I got onto the germination and blooming records. There would soon be some new cards to add to the collection, with the bank balance where it now was.

When the doorbell rang at 5:55 and I took my feet down from the desk and went to see, there was Inspector Cramer.

That broke a precedent. Knowing Wolfe's schedule as

he does, he may come at 11:01 or 6:01, but never at
5:55. Did it mean he wanted five minutes with me first?
It didn't. When I let him in, all I got was a grunt as he
went by, and when I joined him in the office he was in
the red leather chair, his hat on the stand, his feet planted
flat, and his jaw set. Not a word. I went to my chair, sat,
planted my feet flat, and set my jaw. We were like that
when Wolfe came in. As he passed the red leather chair
he grunted, a perfect match for the grunt Cramer had
given me. In his own chair, his bulk adjusted satisfacto-
rily, he grunted again and asked, "How long have you
been here?"

Cramer nodded. "So you can ride Goodwin for not
telling you. Sure. You ride him, and he needles you. A
damn good act. I've seen it often enough, so don't waste
it on me. You lied to me yesterday morning. You said
you had an idea where the money was. Nuts. You *knew*
where it was. How did you know?"

Wolfe's brows were up. "Have you shifted from homicide to kidnaping?"

"No. If you knew where it was you knew who put it
there. It must have been Jimmy Vail. He died Wednesday
night. You told me yesterday that you had no evidence,
either about the whereabouts of the money or Vail's
death. That was a barefaced lie. You used the evidence
about the money to get your paws on it. Now you're
going to use the evidence about Vail's death to pounce on
something else, probably more money. How many times
have I sat here and yapped at you about withholding evidence or obstructing justice?"

"Twenty. Thirty."

"I'm not doing that now. This is different. I'm telling
you that if the evidence you've got about Vail's death is
evidence that he was murdered, and if you refuse to give
it to me here and now, whatever it is I'll dig it up, I'll get
it, and I'll hang an accomplice rap on you and Goodwin
if it's the last thing I do this side of hell."

"Hhmmm," Wolfe said. He turned. "Archie. I have a
good memory, but yours is incomparable. Have we any
shred of evidence regarding the death of Mr. Vail that
Mr. Cramer lacks?"

I shook my head. "No, sir. He probably has a good

deal, little details, that we lack." I turned to Cramer. "Look. I certainly know everything that Mr. Wolfe knows. But yesterday he not only told you that he was convinced that Vail was murdered, I'm with him on that, he also said he was all but certain that he knew who had killed him. I'm not. Certain, my eye. I'd have to pick it out of a hat."

"He didn't say that. That was a question."

Wolfe snorted. "A question only rhetorically. You said I was grandstanding—your word. Apparently you no longer think so, which isn't surprising, since I have found the money. In effect, you are now demanding that I do your interpreting for you."

"That's another lie. I am not."

"But you are." Wolfe turned a palm up. "Consider. As I told you yesterday, my conclusions about the whereabouts of the money and Mr. Vail's death were based on deductions and assumptions from the evidence at hand, and I have no evidence that you do not have. Yesterday you said you would leave me to my deductions and assumptions. Now you want them. You demand them, snarling a threat."

"You're twisting it around as usual. I didn't snarl."

"I'm clarifying it. I am under no necessity, either as a citizen or as a licensed detective, to share the product of my ratiocination with you. I am not obliged to describe the mental process by which I located the money and identified the murderer of Miss Utley and Mr. Vail. I may decide to do so, but it rests with my discretion. I shall consider it, and if and when,—"

The doorbell rang. As I went to the hall I was considering whether it was Andrew Frost with a legal chip on his shoulder or some journalist after crumbs. It was neither. It was Ben Dykes of Westchester County and a stranger. It might or might not be desirable to let them join the party, so I only opened the door to the two-inch crack the chain permitted and spoke through it. "Back again?"

"With bells on," Dykes said.

"You're Archie Goodwin?" the stranger asked. He showed a buzzer, not Westchester. New York. "Open up."

"It's after office hours," I said. "Give me three good reasons why I should—"

"Take a look at the bells," Dykes said and stuck a paper through the crack.

I took it, unfolded it, and looked. Thoroughly. It was a little wordy and high-flown, but I got the idea. "Mr. Wolfe will want to see this," I said. "He's a great reader. Excuse me a minute." I went to the office, waited until Wolfe finished a sentence, and told him, "Sorry to interrupt. Ben Dykes from Westchester with a New York dick for an escort, and with this." I showed the paper. "A court order that Archie Goodwin is to be arrested and held on a charge of grand larceny. On a complaint by Mrs. Althea Vail. It's called a warrant." I turned to Cramer. "Got any more questions before I leave?"

He didn't even glance at me. His eyes were fastened on Wolfe, who had just said that he had identified a murderer. Wolfe put out a hand, and I gave him the paper, and he read it. "She's an imbecile," he declared. "Bring them in."

"We don't need Goodwin," Cramer said. "You'll have him out on bail in the morning."

"Bring them," Wolfe snapped.

I returned to the front, removed the chain, pulled the door open, invited them in, and was surprised to see that there were three of them. Presumably the third one had stayed at the foot of the steps as a reserve in case I started shooting. You've got to use tactics when you go for a gorilla. I soon discovered how wrong I was when they followed me to the office and the third one darted by me to Wolfe's desk, whipped a paper from a pocket, and shoved it at Wolfe. "For you," he said and wheeled and was going, but Ben Dykes caught his arm and demanded, "Who are you?"

"Jack Duffy, process server," he said and jerked loose and trotted out.

"A goddam paper boy," Dykes said disgustedly. I stepped to the hall, saw that he shut the door as he went, and stepped back in. Wolfe had picked up the document and was scowling at it. He read it through, let it fall to the desk, leaned back, closed his eyes, and pushed his lips out. In a moment he pulled them in, then out, in, out . . .

Dykes said, "All right, Goodwin, let's go." The New York dick had suddenly recognized Inspector Cramer and was trying to catch his eye so he could salute, but Cramer was staring at Wolfe. In a minute Wolfe opened his eyes, straightened up, and asked his expert on women, me, "Is she a lunatic?" He tapped the document. "This is a summons. She is suing me, not only for the money in the suitcase, but also to recover the fee she paid me."

"*That* hurts you," Cramer growled.

Wolfe regarded him. "Mr. Cramer, I have a proposal. I would prefer not to describe it for other ears, and I think you share that preference. It is within the discretion of the police to postpone service of a warrant of arrest if it is thought desirable. I suggest that you advise Mr. Dykes, who is accompanied by a member of your force, to wait until tomorrow noon to take Mr. Goodwin into custody. After they leave I'll make my proposal."

Cramer cocked his head and screwed his lips. He had to pretend to give it a hard look, but actually there was nothing to it. By now he knew darned well that Wolfe wasn't grandstanding. He spoke. "Dykes is from Westchester. He has a New York man with him for courtesy, but the arrest is up to him." His head turned. "What about it, Dykes? Would you have to phone White Plains?"

Dykes shook his head. "That wouldn't be necessary, Inspector. I'm supposed to use my head."

"All right, use it. You heard what Wolfe said. If it's just a stall, you can take Goodwin tomorrow."

Dykes hesitated. "If you don't mind, Inspector, I'd like to be able to say that you made it a request."

"Then say it. It's a request."

Dykes went to Wolfe's desk and picked up the warrant, then turned to me. "You won't leave the state, Goodwin."

I told him I wouldn't dream of it, and he headed out, followed by the dick, who never had got to salute Cramer. I got in front of them, wanting to be polite to a man who had postponed tossing me in the can, and let them out. When I returned to the office Wolfe was speaking.

". . . but I must first satisfy myself. As I told you, I

have no evidence. Mr. Goodwin has already been served with a warrant, and I have been served with a summons, and I prefer not to expose myself to an action for libel."

"Nuts. Telling me privately, libel?"

"It's conceivable. But in candor, that's not the main point. I intend to take a certain step, and it's highly likely that if I told you what I have deduced and assumed you would make it extremely difficult for me to take it, if not impossible. You wouldn't dare to take it yourself because, like me, you would have no evidence. You'll hear from me, probably tonight, and by tomorrow noon at the latest." ·

Cramer was anything but pleased. "This is a hell of a proposal."

"It's the best I can do." Wolfe looked at the clock. "I would like to proceed."

"Sure you would." Cramer reached for his hat and put it on. "I should have let Dykes take Goodwin. I'd sleep better if I knew he was in a cell." He rose. "You'd have had to take your certain step anyway." He moved and, halfway to the door, turned. "If you call me tomorrow and say you've decided that your deductions and assumptions were wrong, God help you." He went. That time my going to see that the hall was empty when the door closed wasn't just routine; he might really have stayed inside to get a line on the certain step. As I stepped back in Wolfe snapped, "Get Mrs. Vail."

That wasn't so simple. First I got a female, and after some insisting I got Ralph Purcell. After more insisting he told me to hold the wire, and after a wait I had him again, saying that his sister wouldn't speak with Nero Wolfe or me either. I asked if he would give her a message, and he said yes, and I told him to tell her that Wolfe wanted to tell her how he had known the money was in the house. That did it. After another wait her voice came.

"This is Althea Vail. Nero Wolfe?"

He was at his phone. "Yes. I am prepared to tell you how I knew where the money was, but it's possible that your telephone is tapped. I am also—"

"Why on earth would it be tapped?"

"The pervasive curiosity of the police. I am also prepared to tell you various other things. Examples: the name of the man to whom you gave the suitcase on Iron Mine Road; how I know that there was no Mr. Knapp; the reason why Mr. Vail had to be killed. I shall expect you at my office at nine o'clock this evening."

Silence. She hadn't hung up, but the silence lasted so long that I thought she had left the phone. So long that Wolfe finally asked, "Are you there, madam?"

"Yes." More silence, but after half a minute: "I'll come now."

"No. It will take some time and would run into the dinner hour. Nine o'clock."

"I'll be there." The connection went.

We hung up, and I turned to Wolfe. "What's all the hurry? You haven't got a single solitary scrap."

He was glaring at the phone and switched it to me. "I will not have you carted off to jail on a complaint by that silly wretch. It should be worth keeping. Is that thing in order?"

"I suppose so. It was the last time we used it."

"Test it."

I got up, slipped my hand in between my desk and the wall, and flipped a switch. Then I went and sat in the red leather chair and said in a fairly low voice, "Nero Wolfe is going to put on a charade, and let us hope he doesn't break a leg." I went to my desk and turned it off, then went to the kitchen, opened a cupboard door, did some manipulating, and flipped a switch, and in a few seconds my voice came out: "Nero Wolfe is going to put on a charade, and let us hope he doesn't break a leg." I reached in and turned it off, returned to the office, and reported, "It's okay. Anything else?"

"Yes. That idiot may have a gun or a bomb or heaven knows what. Stay near her."

"Or she may have a lawyer."

"No. No indeed. She's not that big an idiot." He picked up the summons and scowled at it.

15

She came at 8:50, ten minutes ahead of time. I was getting Wolfe's okay on a change in the program when the doorbell rang. In order to stay near her I would have had to sit in one of the yellow chairs near the red leather chair, and I prefer to be at my desk, or I would have had to put her in one of the yellow chairs near me, and Wolfe prefers to have a caller in the red leather chair because the window is then at his back.

It was a pleasant May Day evening, and she had no wrap over her tailored suit, so the only problem was her handbag—a big black leather one with a trick clasp. I learned about the clasp when I tried to open it, after I had got it from her lap and taken it to my desk. Her reaction to my snatching it, which I did as soon as she was seated and had no hand on it, showed the condition of her nerves. She made no sound and no movement, but merely stared at me as I took it to my desk, and she said nothing while I fiddled with it, finding the trick clasp and opening it, and inspected the contents. Nothing in it seemed to be menacing, and when I went and put it back on her lap she had transferred the stare to Wolfe. I might have felt a little sorry for her if it hadn't been for the warrant that Ben Dykes would be back with at noon tomorrow. When you grab a woman's bag and open it and go through it, and all she does is sit and stare, she could certainly use a little sympathy.

There was no sympathy in Wolfe's expression as he regarded her. "This isn't an inquisition, Mrs. Vail," he said. "I have no questions to ask you. It will be a monologue, not a tête-à-tête, and it will be prolonged. I advise you to say nothing whatever."

"I wouldn't answer any questions if you did ask them," she said. Her voice was good enough. "You said there was no Mr. Knapp. That's crazy."

"Not as crazy as your invention of him." Wolfe leaned back. "This will be easier to follow if I begin in the middle. Mr. Goodwin has told you how I reached the conclusion that your husband was murdered. That didn't help much unless I could identify the murderer, and as a first step I needed to see those who were at that gathering Wednesday evening. Let's take them in the order in which I saw them.

"First, your son. When he came to hire me to find the money for him I suggested the possibility that he had had a hand in the kidnaping and knew where the money was, that he couldn't very well just go and get it, and that he intended to supply hints that would lead to its discovery by me—or by Mr. Goodwin. When I made that suggestion at the beginning of our conversation, I thought it was a real possibility, but by the time our talk ended I had discarded it. For such a finesse a subtle and agile mind would be needed, and also a ready tongue. Such a witling as your son couldn't possibly have conceived it, much less execute it. So he had come to me in good faith; he hadn't been involved in the kidnaping; he didn't know where the money was; and he hadn't killed Mr. Vail."

"You said you would tell me how you knew there was no Mr. Knapp."

"That will come in its place. Second, your daughter. But you may not know even now what led Mr. Goodwin and me to suspect that Dinah Utley was a party to the kidnaping. Do you?"

"No."

"Your brother hasn't told you?"

"No."

"Nor the police?"

"No."

"The note that came in the mail. It had been typed by her. I won't elucidate that; this will take long enough without such details. When Mr. Goodwin saw that the other two notes which you had found in telephone books —I know now, of course, that they were not in the books, you had them with you and went to the books and pretended to find them—when Mr. Goodwin saw that they too had been typed by her, the suspicion became a conclusion. And ten minutes' talk with your daughter made it manifest that it was quite impossible that she had been allied with Dinah Utley in any kind of enterprise, let alone one as ambitious and hazardous as kidnaping. Your daughter is a vulgarian, a dunce, and a snob. Also she had come to demand that I find the money for her, but even without that it was plain that she, like her brother, had not been involved in the kidnaping; she didn't know where the money was; and she hadn't killed Mr. Vail.

"Third, your brother. From Mr. Goodwin's report of his behavior Wednesday afternoon, or rather, his lack of behavior, his silence, I had tentatively marked him as the one who most needed watching. After twenty minutes with him, him in the chair you are in now, I had to conclude that it was impossible. You know his habit of looking at A when B starts to speak."

"Yes."

"His explanation of that habit was enough. A man with a reaction so hopelessly out of control cannot have effective and sustained control over any of his faculties. He would never trust himself to undertake an operation that required audacity, ingenuity, and mettle. There were many other indications. His parting words were 'I guess I *am* a fool,' and he meant them. Patently he was not the man.

"Fourth, Andrew Frost. As you know, he came yesterday morning, but I learned nothing from that interview. There was nothing in his words or tone or manner to challenge the possibility that he was the culprit, and, except for you, that was the only possibility that remained. But through an assistant I had already learned enough about him to exclude him—his record, his position in his profession and in society, his financial status. That didn't exclude him as a possible murderer, but it was inconceivable that he had been involved in the kidnaping. He would have had to conspire with at least two others, Miss Utley and Mr. Knapp, and probably more, with the only objective in view a share of the loot, and therefore he would have been at their mercy, in mortal danger indefinitely. What if one of his confederates had been caught and had talked? To suppose that such a man had incurred such a risk for such a return? No."

Wolfe shook his head. "No. Therefore it was you. You had been a party to the kidnaping, you had killed Dinah Utley, and you had killed your husband. I reached that conclusion at ten o'clock Saturday evening, but I wanted to see Mr. Frost before I acted on it. It was barely possible that after talking with him I would reconsider my decision about him. I didn't. Will you have some refreshment? A drink? Coffee?"

No reply. No movement.

"Tell me if you want something. I'll have some beer." He pushed a button and leaned back again. "Also before I acted on it I had to examine it. I had to satisfy myself that no fact and no factor known to me rendered it untenable; and first came motive. What conceivable reason could you have had for getting half a million dollars in cash from your bank and going through that elaborate rigmarole to deliver it to a masked man at an isolated spot on a country road at midnight, other than your ostensible reason? Please bear in mind, Mrs. Vail, that from here on I am not reporting; I am only telling you how I satisfied myself. If in this instance or that I chose the wrong alternative you may correct me, but I still advise you to say nothing."

I never saw advice better followed. She had a good opportunity to speak, for Fritz came with beer, and Wolf poured, but she didn't take advantage of it. He waited for the foam to sink to the proper level, then lifted the glass and drank.

He leaned back. "I found only one acceptable answer. The man you delivered the suitcase to was your husband. He probably was masked, for both you and he gave meticulous attention to detail throughout the operation. Very well; why? What were you accomplishing? You were establishing the fact that you had suffered a loss of half a million dollars, and that fact would net you ninety-one per cent of the half a million, since you would deduct it as a casualty on your income-tax report. I haven't inquired as to whether such a casualty would be deductible, and I don't suppose you did, probably you merely assumed that it would be. If your income for the year would be less than half a million, no matter; you could carry the loss back for three previous years and forward for five future years. Well worth the effort, surely."

He came forward to drink, then back again. "Other facts and factors. Why did you and your husband bring Dinah Utley into it? You couldn't plan it to your satisfaction without her. Take one detail, the phone call from

Mr. Knapp. You wanted no doubt whatever in any quarter that the kidnaping was genuine, and you thought there
must be a phone call. Mr. Vail couldn't make it, for even
if he disguised his voice it might be recognized. It would
be simpler and safer to use Miss Utley, your trusted em-
ployee, than to have some man, no matter who, make the
call. Of course the call was never made. Miss Utley not
only typed the notes; she also typed the transcript of the
supposed conversation on the phone. I presume her re-
ward was to be a modest share of the booty.

"Was it you or your husband who conceived the notion
—No. I said I would ask you no questions. All the same,
it's an interesting point, which of you thought of coming
to me, since that was what led to disaster. No doubt it
seemed to be an excellent stroke in your elaborate plans
to achieve verisimilitude; not only coming to me but also
the hocus-pocus about getting here; ten thousand dollars
wasn't much to pay for establishing that you were desper-
ately concerned for your husband's safety. You couldn't
foresee that I would insist on seeing your secretary, but
when I made that demand your check was already on my
desk, and you didn't dare take it back merely because I
wished to speak with Miss Utley. Nor could you foresee
that I would propose a step that would expose me to the
risk of an extended and expensive operation, and that I
would demand an additional sum as insurance against
possible loss. You didn't like that at all. Your teeth bit
into your lip as you wrote the check, but you had to.
Fifty thousand dollars makes a substantial hole in half a
million, but you had made it so clear that nothing mat-
tered but your husband's safety, certainly money didn't,
that you couldn't very well refuse."

He poured beer, drank when the foam was right, and
went on. "I don't know if you regretted that you had
come to me when you left, but you certainly did later,
when Miss Utley returned after seeing me. As I said, I'm
not reporting, I'm telling you how I satisfied myself. I got an
inkling of Miss Utley's temperament and character when
she was here, and more than an inkling from what your
brother told me about her. From questions Mr. Goodwin
and I asked her, and from our taking her fingerprints, she
became apprehensive. She feared that you had somehow

aroused my suspicion, that I suspected her, and that I might disclose the fraud; and when she returned she tried to persuade you to give it up. You wouldn't. All the preliminaries had been performed; you had the money in the suitcase; you had given me sixty thousand dollars; all that remained was the consummation. You tried to remove Miss Utley's fears, to convince her that there was no danger of exposure, and you thought you succeeded, but you didn't.

"Shortly before eight o'clock you left in your car with the suitcase in the trunk, not knowing that, instead of subsiding, Miss Utley's alarm had grown. An hour after your departure she took the typewriter from the house, put it in her car, and drove to the country. Here there are alternatives; either is acceptable; I prefer this one: after disposing of the typewriter she intended to go to where Mr. Vail was in hiding, arriving before he left for the rendezvous with you, describe the situation, and insist that the project be abandoned. But something intervened, probably the difficulty of disposing of the typewriter unseen in a spot where it would surely never be found, and to see Mr. Vail she had to go to Iron Mine Road, which had been named in one of the notes she had typed."

Wolfe drank beer. "Some of what I have said is conjectural, but this is not. Miss Utley got to Iron Mine Road before you did. When you and your husband arrived, you in your car and he in his, she told him of her fears and insisted that the project must be abandoned. He didn't agree. He didn't stay long to debate it; he was supposed to be concealed somewhere by kidnapers, and even in that secluded spot there was a possibility that someone might come along. He put the suitcase in his car and drove off, leaving it to you to deal with her, and you tried to, but she wouldn't be persuaded. She may have demanded a large share of the half million to offset the risk, but I doubt it. From what your brother said of her it's more likely that she was filled with dismay. Either she made it plain that she would wreck the project by disclosing it, or you were convinced that she intended to. Infuriated, you assaulted her. You hit her on the head with something—a handy rock?—and as she lay unconscious you got in her car and ran it over her, nosed the car into an opening, dragged the body to the ditch and rolled it in, got in your car, and drove away. If, ignoring my advice to say nothing, you ask why I say that you, not Mr. Vail, killed her, I repeat that I had to satisfy myself. If he killed her, why was he killed the next day? There was no tenable answer.

"To satisfy myself it wasn't necessary to supply answers to all relevant questions. For example, where was your husband from Sunday to Wednesday morning? I don't know and need not bother to guess, but since other details were carefully and thoroughly planned I assume that one was too. It had to be some spot where both he and his car could be effectively concealed, especially in the daytime. Of course you had to know where it was, since something might happen that would make it necessary to alter the plan. No doubt you and he chose the spot with great care and deliberation. Wherever it was, probably it lacked the convenience of a telephone, so he had to get to one Tuesday evening in order to make the calls to Fowler's Inn and The Fatted Calf, but that was after dark, and of course that detail too was prudently contrived.

"For another example of questions that can be left open, why did you tell your son he could have the money if he found it? Why not? Knowing yourself where it was, you knew he wouldn't find it. Still another example, why did you and your husband insist on keeping silent about the kidnaping for forty-eight hours after he returned home? A good guess is that you wanted enough time to pass to make sure that no trail had been left, but it doesn't have to be verified for my satisfaction. Regarding any known fact or factor I need only establish that it doesn't contradict my deduction—my final deduction, that you killed your husband. As for his coming to see me Wednesday morning, posthaste after his return, it would have been surprising if he hadn't. He wanted to learn how much ground there was, if any, for Miss Utley's fears; what he learned, over the telephone from you, was that she was dead; and he departed, again posthaste, to go to you.

"He knew, of course, that you had killed Dinah Utley, and you were completely at his mercy. He couldn't expose you as a murderer without divulging his own complicity in preparations for a swindle, but the swindle hadn't been consummated; there would be no swindle until the deduction had been made on your income-tax return and you and he had signed it. Meanwhile he had a cogent threat, and he used it. He demanded the entire half a million for himself. You were in a pickle. After all the planning, all the exertion, all the painstaking, all the zeal, even after your desperate resort to murder, you were to get nothing. That was not to be borne. Jimmy Vail must die."

A noise came from her, but it wasn't a word; it was merely the kind of involuntary noise that is squeezed out by a blow or a sting. Wolfe went on. "You planned it with the care and foresight you had so admirably demonstrated in planning the kidnaping. You needed a drug, and since you assuredly wouldn't take the risk of procuring one in haste, you must have had one in your possession—probably chloral hydrate, since you may plausibly have had it in some mixture in your medicine cabinet, but that's another question I may leave open. Either luck was with you Wednesday evening, or you knew him so well that you could safely calculate that when drowsiness overtook him from the drug you had put in his drink he would die on the couch instead of going to his room. For the rest you needed no luck. After Mr. Frost left you went down to the library, found your husband in a coma as you had a right to expect, dragged him across to the desired spot, and toppled the statue on him. With your marked talent for detail, undoubtedly you took his feet. Shoes dragged along a floor will leave telltale marks, even on a rug, but a head and shoulders won't. Certainly you didn't leave it to luck whether the statue would land where you wanted it. You wiggled it to learn its direction of least resistance. Evidently the thump wasn't heard, because the inmates were all in upper rooms; and the statue didn't hit the floor, the main impact was on your husband's chest, and it would have been more of a crunch than a thump."

Wolfe straightened up, took in air through his nose as far down as it could do, and let it out through his mouth. His eyes narrowed at her. "Mrs. Vail," he said, "I confess

that I am not without animus. I have been provoked by
the suit you have served against me, and by your complaint against Mr. Goodwin, subjecting him to arrest on a
criminal charge. But even so I would hesitate to upbraid
you on moral grounds for the fraud you conceived and
tried to execute. Millions of your fellow citizens will cheat
on their income tax this year. Nor would I reproach you
without qualification for killing Miss Utley; you did it in
the instant heat of uncontrollable passion. But killing
your husband is another matter. That was planned and
premeditated and ruthlessly executed; and for a sordid
end. Merely for money. You killed him in cold blood because he was going to deprive you of the fruit of your
swindle. That, I submit, was execrable. That would be
condemned even by—"

"That's not true," she said. It barely got out through
her tight throat, and she repeated it. "That's not true!"

"I advised you to say nothing, madam. That would be
condemned even—"

"But it's not true! It wasn't the money!" She was grip-
ping the chair arms. "He could have had the money. I
told him he could. He wouldn't. It was Dinah. He was
going to leave me because I had—because of Dinah. That
was why—it wasn't the money."

"I prefer it that he demanded the money."

"No!"

"He threatened to expose you as a murderer?"

"No. He said he wouldn't. But he was going to leave
me, and I loved him." Her mouth worked, and her fingers
clawed at the chair arms, scratching at the leather. "I
loved him, and he was going to leave me."

"And of course that might mean your exposure."
Wolfe's voice was low, down almost to a murmur. "Away
from you, no longer enjoying your bounty, there was no
telling what he might do. So he had to die. I offer you my
apology. I concede that your end was not sordid, that you
were in mortal danger. Did you try to gull him, did you
deny that you had killed Dinah Utley?"

"No, he knew I had." She made fists. "I was insane, I
must have been. You're right, I knew what would happen
if he left me, but that wasn't it. I must have been insane.

Later that night I went down to the library again and stayed there with him until—"

She jerked up straight. "What am I saying? What did I say?"

"Enough." Not a murmur. "You said what I expected you to say when I accused you of killing your husband merely for money. That was absurd, but no more absurd than your attack on Mr. Goodwin and me after we found the money. You intended, of course, to put the onus on your deceased husband—to have it inferred that he had arranged the kidnaping to get the money for himself, with Dinah Utley as an accomplice, that he had killed her, and possibly even that he had killed himself through fear or remorse, though that would be rather farfetched—a man would hardly choose that method of committing suicide. But you should have known that you would arouse—"

He stopped because his audience was walking out on him. When she shifted her feet to get up, her bag slipped to the floor, and I went and picked it up and handed it to her and followed her out. Having circled around her in the hall to get in front, I had the door open by the time she reached it, and I went out to the stoop to watch her go down the steps. If she went home and finished up the chloral hydrate, that would be her funeral, but I didn't want her stumbling and breaking her neck on our premises. She wasn't any too steady, but she made it to the sidewalk and turned right, and I went back in.

Going to the kitchen, I got the tape and the playback from the cupboard and took them to the office. Wolfe sat and scowled at me as I got things ready, switched it on, ran it through to what might be the spot, and turned on the sound. Wolfe's voice came.

". . . in the instant heat of uncontrollable passion. But killing your husband is another matter. That was planned and premeditated and ruthlessly executed; and for a sordid end. Merely for money. You killed him in cold blood because he was going to deprive you of the fruit of your swindle. That, I submit, was execrable. That would be condemned even by—"

"That's not true. That's not true!"

"I advised you to say nothing, madam. That would be condemned even—"

"But it's not true! It wasn't the money! He could have had the money. I told him he could. He wouldn't. It was Dinah. He was going to leave me because I had—because of Dinah. That was why—it wasn't the money."

It went on to the end, good and clear, as it should have been, since that installation had cost twelve hundred smackers. As I turned it off Wolfe said, "Satisfactory. Take it to Mr. Cramer."

"Now?"

"Yes. That wretch may be dead within the hour. If he isn't at his office, have him summoned. I don't want him storming in here tomorrow to bark at me for delaying delivery of a confession of a murderer."

I reached for the tape.

16

She not only wasn't dead within the hour; she's not dead yet. That was three months ago, and last week a jury of eight men and four women stayed hung for fifty-two hours and then gave up. It stood seven for conviction of first-degree murder and five for acquittal. Whether this report gets published or not depends on the jury at the second trial. If it hangs too, or acquits, the script will have to go into a locked drawer in my room, with several others to keep it company.

If you care about whether I took another trip to White Plains, I did—Tuesday noon, escorted by Ben Dykes. By then Mrs. Vail had been taken to the District Attorney's office, but everyone was too busy to worry about me. I was out on bail by five o'clock, but I had had my fingerprints taken for the nineteenth time. It took a week before the charge was quashed, and the cost of the bail cut Wolfe's hundred grand down to $99,925. Even so, I'm having plenty of time to go for walks, getting angles on people and things. Having reached that bracket by the first of May, Wolfe relaxed and has stayed relaxed. If you offered him ten thousand bucks to detect who swiped your hat at a cocktail party yesterday he wouldn't even bother to glare at you.